William McLaughlin

Ceremonies Connected with the Unveiling of the Bronze

Statue

of Gen. Thomas J. Stonewall Jackson, at Lexington

William McLaughlin

Ceremonies Connected with the Unveiling of the Bronze Statue
of Gen. Thomas J. Stonewall Jackson, at Lexington

ISBN/EAN: 9783337224967

Printed in Europe, USA, Canada, Australia, Japan

Cover: Foto ©Andreas Hilbeck / pixelio.de

More available books at **www.hansebooks.com**

GEN. THOMAS J. (STONEWALL) JACKSON.

CEREMONIES

CONNECTED WITH THE

UNVEILING OF THE BRONZE STATUE

OF

GEN. THOMAS J. (STONEWALL) JACKSON,

AT

LEXINGTON, VIRGINIA,

JULY 21st, 1891.

BY

WILLIAM McLAUGHLIN,

A Member of the Executive Committee of the Jackson Memorial Association.

———————————

BALTIMORE:

JOHN MURPHY & CO.

1891.

CONTENTS.

HISTORICAL SKETCH

JACKSON MEMORIAL ASSOCIATION.

The movement for the erection of a monument at the grave of Lieutenant-General Thomas J. (Stonewall) Jackson had its inception in a meeting, at the house of Adjutant William W. Lewis in Lexington, in January, 1875, of Confederate soldiers who had served under Jackson.

It was determined to inaugurate the movement, the corporators were selected, and Col. Charles A. Davidson, who had served as an officer of the First Virginia Battalion, was appointed a committee to prepare a charter and have it enacted into a law by the General Assembly of Virginia. Such a charter was prepared and became a law on the 8th day of March, 1875. It incorporated James K. Edmondson, William W. Lewis, Charles A. Davidson, James J. White, Alexander T. Barclay, William A. Anderson, John C. Boude, John T. Sayers, John W. Lyell, William F. Johnston, William McLaughlin, Henry K. Douglass, Robert W. Hunter, Samuel J. C. Moore, Asher W. Harman, Thomas D. Ranson, George G. Grattan, James A. Walker, Hunter H. McGuire, James P. Smith, George G. Junkin, John H. B. Jones, David E. Moore, James L. White, Calvin M. Dold, and such other persons as they should associate with them, by the name and style of the Jackson Memorial Association.

5

The objects and purposes of this corporation were declared to be " to erect a suitable monument over the grave of Lieutenant-General Thomas J. Jackson, and such other monuments as it may be determined to erect in perpetuation of his memory, and to purchase and beautify grounds for the location of such monuments," and the Association was invested with all the powers of a corporation. The corporators named were constituted the Executive Committee of the Association, with power to increase the number of the committee, to fill the offices of the corporation, and to fill any vacancies that might occur in their body by death or otherwise.

Soon after the charter was obtained some money was contributed, but at a conference of the resident incorporators it was ascertained that most of those who would be active members of this Association were also active members of the Lee Memorial Association ; and as that Association was earnestly engaged in erecting a suitable monument to General Robert E. Lee, it was thought best to defer the work of this Association until that was accomplished. The beautiful recumbent statue of General Robert E. Lee by Valentine was placed in position over his remains in a mausoleum attached to the chapel of Washington and Lee University, and unveiled with imposing ceremonies on the 28th day of June, 1883.

This being done it was determined to commence the work of the Jackson Memorial Association. A meeting for the purpose of organizing for active work was held at Lexington on the fifth day of September, 1883. There were present at this meeting William McLaughlin, John W. Lyell, James K. Edmondson, Thomas D. Ranson, David E. Moore, C. M. Dold and John C. Boude. John C. Boude was elected Secretary, and Charles M. Figgat Treasurer of the Association. It was " resolved that the Association endeavor to raise a sufficient sum to be expended in a suitable monument to be erected at the grave of General Thomas J. Jackson in the cemetery at Lexington, Virginia." Another meeting was held on the 13th of September, 1883, to complete the organization under the charter, when General G. W. C. Lee was elected President of the Jackson Memorial Association, and Col. James K. Edmondson Chairman of the Executive Committee. It appearing that Col.

Charles A. Davidson had departed this life, and that William W. Lewis had removed from the State, Col. Edmund Pendleton and James D. Anderson were elected to fill these vacancies.

The organization of the Jackson Memorial Association was as follows, it being worthy of note that no further vacancies for any cause occurred during the eight years of its active work :

President.

MAJOR-GENERAL G. W. C. LEE, C. S. A.

Executive Committee.

COL. JAMES K. EDMONDSON, 27th Va. Inf., *Chairman.*
MAJ.-GEN. JAMES A. WALKER, C. S. A.
COL. JOHN W. LYELL, 47th Va. Inf.
COL. ASHER W. HARMAN, 12th Va. Cav.
COL. EDMUND PENDLETON, 15th La. Inf.
HUNTER H. McGUIRE, Medical Director 2d Corps, A. N. V.
LT.-COL. WILLIAM McLAUGHLIN, Artillery, C. S. A.
LT.-COL. HENRY K. DOUGLASS, Staff of 2d Corps, A. N. V.
MAJ. ROBERT W. HUNTER, Asst. Adjt.-Gen. 2d Corps, A. N.V.
MAJ. S. J. C. MOORE, Asst. Adjt.-Gen. 2d Corps, A. N. V.
MAJ. GEORGE G. JUNKIN, Virginia Cavalry.
CAPT. JAMES J. WHITE, 4th Va. Inf.
JOHN T. SAYERS, Surgeon 4th Va. Inf.
CAPT. JAMES P. SMITH, Aid to Gen. Jackson.
CAPT. JOHN C. BOUDE, 27th Va. Inf.
CAPT. GEORGE G. GRATTAN, Asst. Adjt.-Gen. Colquitt's Brigade.
CAPT. JAMES L. WHITE, Asst. Adjt.-Gen. Stonewall Brigade.
ENSIGN ALEX. T. BARCLAY, 4th Va. Inf.
LT. J. H. B. JONES, 4th Va. Inf.
SERGT.-MAJ. THOMAS D. RANSON, 52d Va. Inf.
SERGT. DAVID E. MOORE, Rockbridge Artillery.
OR.-SERGT. WILLIAM A. ANDERSON, 4th Va. Inf.
OR.-SERGT. JAMES D. ANDERSON, 25th Va. Inf.
WILLIAM F. JOHNSTON, Rockbridge Artillery.
CALVIN M. DOLD, Rockbridge Artillery.

On the 31st day of December, 1884, the Executive Committee issued an appeal to "the Comrades and Countrymen of Stonewall Jackson" for aid in the enterprise they had undertaken. The following is an extract from the address:

"More than twenty years have passed since the death of Gen. T. J. JACKSON, and the spot where he lies buried is unmarked, save by the simple stone placed there from limited means by his devoted wife.

"We well know that he needs no monument. His grand figure will loom up in history, though this generation pass away and leave no sign of its appreciation of his virtues and his greatness.

"But the men among whom he lived, moved and earned immortality; the people whose cause he illustrated by his prowess and vindicated by his noble Christian life and heroic death; the surviving soldiers of the brigade, division and corps whom he led and loved, and whose names are linked with his to immortal renown, should not go down to their graves without leaving some enduring memorial of their affection for him, and their admiration for his splendid achievements and character.

"In this spirit the 'JACKSON MEMORIAL ASSOCIATION,' consisting of soldiers who served under and with General Jackson, has been organized under a charter granted by the State of Virginia.

"The object of the Association is to erect at the grave of our beloved leader a monument commemorative of the love and veneration in which his countrymen cherish his memory.

"The Association and its object have the sympathy and approval of the honored widow of our dead chieftain, as will be seen from her letter, a copy of which is annexed to this address."

The letter of Mrs. Jackson referred to is as follows:

"RICHMOND, VA., *October* 22d, 1884.

" COL. J. K. EDMONDSON.

"*Dear Sir*,—I am greatly gratified to learn that the object of the 'Jackson Memorial Association' is to erect a monument over the grave of my husband in the cemetery at Lexington.

" You were kind enough to suggest that some expression of my approval of this design would aid in its accomplishment. If so, permit me to say the organization, with its corps of officers, seems to me to be all that could be desired, and I will await with the deepest interest the result of this purpose to do honor to the name and memory of General Jackson.

" Faithfully yours,

M. A. JACKSON."

The appeal was responded to from different parts of the country. William W. Corcoran, the eminent philanthropist, subscribed $1,000. Agents were sent out who met with moderate success. Handsome contributions, however, were received from Charleston, Columbia, and Greenville, S. C., Charlestown, West Va., and Staunton, Va. The latter embraced $182.50, the proceeds of a lecture delivered by Col. William Allan.

In December, 1885, a number of ladies of Lexington were invited to meet at the Franklin Hall to organize for the purpose of raising funds in aid of the monument fund. At the appointed time seven ladies met and were addressed by Col. Edmondson. After a short conference they determined to have a bazaar and concert, and to direct all their energies to the accomplishment of the object which met their hearty approval. They adjourned until the second of January, 1886, when a large number of ladies attended and formed The Ladies' Jackson Memorial Association, for the purpose of aiding this laudable cause.

The organization of the Association was as follows :

MISS MARY V. KIRKPATRICK, *President.*
MISS EDMONIA P. WADDELL, *Vice-President.*
MISS MERCER WILLIAMSON, *Secretary.*
MRS. E. A. DUNCAN, *Treasurer.*

Executive Committee.

Mrs. S. P. Lee,	Mrs. James J. White,
Mrs. J. B. Tayler,	Mrs. T. L. Preston,
Mrs. E. Duval,	Mrs. W. T. Jewell,
Mrs. A. L. Nelson,	Mrs. S. Pitzer,

Miss Susan Parks,	Mrs. J. Willis,
Mrs. G. P. Chalkley,	Mrs. Charles M. Figgat,
Miss Annie R. White,	Mrs. H. Davin,
Miss Madge Paxton,	Mrs. J. Evans,
Mrs. J. A. Jackson,	Mrs. J. W. Lyell,
Mrs. A. D. Estill,	Mrs. J. K. Edmondson.
Miss Nannie Brady,	

The Association went actively to work preparing for the bazaar, and the ladies of the town engaged in it with their whole hearts. Contributions in money, supplies, and fancy articles were solicited in the northern and western cities, and in Virginia and the South, and the appeals met with a gratifying response. The bazaar was held in February, 1886, in the buildings of the Ann Smith Academy, which were generously tendered by Miss Madge Paxton, the Principal. It lasted for a week, and, although the weather was very bad, was liberally patronized. The proceeds amounted to $1,196.05, which, augmented by membership fees and contributions in money, enabled the treasurer, Mrs. E. A. Duncan, to turn over to the Jackson Memorial Association on the 23d of February, 1886, the handsome sum of $2,000. Among the money contributions were $100 from Gen. G. W. C. Lee through Mrs. A. L. Nelson, and a like sum from Gen. J. A. Early through Mrs. J. Wills. Mrs. Duncan, being about to remove from the county, resigned her position as treasurer, and Miss Mary Nelson Pendleton was elected in her place.

The Ladies' Association continued to press their work, and their efforts met a liberal response, and up to April 1st, 1889, they were enabled to turn over to the Jackson Memorial Association the further sum of $3,080.62. This included the $1,000 previously subscribed by Mr. Corcoran and remitted through Mrs. James J. White ; $250 from Mr. Paul Tulane of Princeton, N. J., through Mrs. Margaret J. Preston ; $100 from Col. William P. Thompson, of Cleveland, Ohio, through Miss Edmonia P. Waddell ; $50 from Miss Mildred C. Lee, through Miss Mary V. Kirkpatrick ; $144.10 collected by Mrs. Helen Bruce in Louisville, Ky.; $152 collected by Mrs. A. W. Gaines in Chattanooga, Tenn.; $100 collected by Miss Mamie Echols, a little girl at Balcony Falls, and sent through Mrs. J. K. Edmondson; $63, the proceeds of a lecture in Lexington, by Col. William Allan; and $135.15, the proceeds of a concert given by the Stonewall Brigade Band in the chapel of Washington and Lee University.

The money received by the Jackson Memorial Association was promptly and safely invested.

In April, 1889, the Executive Committee felt that the funds in hand would enable them to commence their work, and that they could safely trust to the liberality of a patriotic people to supply what was wanting to complete it. Accordingly they entered into correspondence with the artist, Edward V. Valentine, who had designed the beautiful recumbent figure of General Robert E. Lee, with reference to a suitable memorial. By invitation he met the Committee on the 8th day of May, 1888. He appeared before the Committee and strongly recommended a bronze statue of heroic size of General Jackson to be placed over his grave as the most fitting memorial. The Committee accepted his suggestion, and at once entered into a contract with Mr. Valentine to model and erect a bronze statue for the sum of $9,000; $1,700 to be paid when the small model was completed and accepted by the Committee, $2,800 when the large model was completed in clay, and $4,500 when the statue in bronze was completed and delivered in Lexington. The work was to be completed in three years, and the 21st day of July, 1891, the thirtieth anniversary of the battle of Manassas, where Jackson won his soubriquet, was selected as the day for the unveiling. When the contract was entered into Mrs. Jackson was informed of what had been done. She replied in the following letter:

"LEXINGTON, VA., *July* 5, 1888.

" COL. J. K. EDMONDSON,
" *Chairman Jackson Memorial Association.*

" *Dear Sir,*—The work of your Association, which I find so advanced as to complete a contract with Mr. Valentine for a bronze portrait statue of Gen. Jackson, meets with my entire and cordial approval, and I shall be most happy to do all in my power to further the success of your laudable and patriotic enterprise in erecting this monument. I must also express my most grateful appreciation of the noble part the ladies of Lexington have taken in assisting you, and wish them and your Association god-speed in the accomplishment of a work so dear and sacred to my heart.

" Faithfully yours,

" M. A. JACKSON, Executrix."

The small model was completed and exhibited to the Committee on the first day of February, 1889, when it was approved and accepted unanimously, the vote being as follows : Gen. G. W. C. Lee, president, Col. James K. Edmondson, chairman, Col. Edmund Pendleton, Capt. J. J. White, Capt. John C. Boude, D. E. Moore, J. D. Anderson, C. M. Dold and A. T. Barclay.

On the first day of March, 1890, the Committee was informed by Mr. Valentine that the clay model was about completed. He requested the Committee to inspect the model preparatory to casting. The Committee requested Dr. Hunter H. McGuire and the Rev. Moses D. Hoge, D. D., who were well acquainted with General Jackson and were well known art critics, to inspect the model and report. They did so and submitted the following report :

" RICHMOND, April 23, 1890.

" J. K. EDMONDSON, ESQ., Chairman of the Executive Committee of the Jackson Memorial Association.

" Dear Sir,—In compliance with your request that we should give you our impressions of the statue of General T. J. Jackson, which is now completed so far as the clay model is concerned, we beg leave to say that we have repeatedly visited the studio of Mr. Valentine while the work was in progress and since it was finished, and we regard it both in conception and in detail equal in merit with the recumbent statue of General Lee.

" It represents Gen. Jackson in an attitude suggestive of strength and determination, looking off into the distance with an expression of quiet confidence.

" The posture is easy and natural, and yet there is a certain dignity in the bearing almost majestic. There is nothing dramatic or exaggerated either in the design or in the execution of the work, but it is one which in our judgment will gratify those who knew

General Jackson, as a good likeness and a noble delineation of the man, while to those who never saw him it will convey an impression which will satisfy the expectation awakened by one whose character and achievements touched the imagination of the world, and created the ideal of a true soldier of the Country and of the Cross.

" MOSES D. HOGE,

" HUNTER McGUIRE."

The report was approved by the Committee, the model was placed in the hands of the moulder, The Henry Bonnard Bronze Company, in New York city, and was completed and safely housed in Lexington in December, 1890.

The Committee continued to solicit contributions, and on the 31st of December, 1889, another circular was issued, from which we make the following extracts.

" More than twenty-six years have passed since General Thomas J. Jackson fell at Chancellorsville, yet the spot where he lies buried is unmarked, save by the simple head-stone placed there by his widow, inscribed only with his name, and obscured by its surroundings.

" We know that he needs no monument. His grand figure will loom up in history though this generation pass away and leave no sign of its appreciation of his virtues and of his greatness.

" But the men among whom he lived and moved and earned immortality ; the people whose cause he illustrated by his prowess and vindicated by his noble Christian life and heroic death ; the surviving soldiers of the brigade, division and corps whom he led and loved, and whose names are linked with his to immortal renown, should not go down to their graves without leaving some enduring memorial of their affection for him, and their admiration for his character and his splendid achievements.

" In this spirit the ' Jackson Memorial Association,' consisting of soldiers who served under and with General Jackson (some of them upon his staff), was organized in 1875 under a charter granted by the State of Virginia, with General G. W. C. Lee as President and Captain John C. Boude, of Lexington, as Secretary.

" Its object was to erect over the remains of our lamented leader a monument worthy to bear that illustrious name, and to acquire grounds suitable for the purpose.

" It is needless to say that his widow approves the purpose thus to do honor to his memory.

" The details of the work have been arranged, and it now approaches completion. A site in all respects suitable was secured in the cemetery at Lexington, near by the grave, sufficient in dimensions and encircled by a carriage drive, commanding a beautiful prospect of the Valley and the Blue Ridge Mountains. A massive pedestal will be erected, of the native gray limestone, with a crypt within to receive the remains, and this surmounted by a standing figure, of heroic size (eight feet), in bronze, which, it is confidently hoped, will be a lifelike resemblance of our dead chieftain, and a work in every respect worthy of the artist's high reputation. The contract for the statue was made with our Virginia sculptor, Valentine, who was fortunately in possession of the death mask, taken while the body lay at Richmond, and has seen his subject. His small model, under the crucial test of exhibition at Lexington, was pronounced a most faithful likeness. The larger one is almost ready for the casting in bronze. The expectation is to have the entire work in place for its inauguration on the 21st July, 1891, the thirtieth anniversary of a memorable day. It will preserve, in material the most enduring, the very features and the form so often seen and cheered at the edge of battle. The figure and the pose are as perfect as the face."

Some contributions were received in response to this circular, but not sufficient to justify the Committee in relying upon these means to raise the requisite balance required. Accordingly they again sought the aid of the Ladies' Memorial Association, and found a warm response. The ladies entered into the object with their former zeal and alacrity, and at once commenced preparations for another bazaar. They also commenced correspondence with admirers of General Jackson all over the country, and were well repaid for their labors. The bazaar was held in the public school building in Lexington, and commenced on the fifteenth of December, 1891. The ladies of the town entered into it with spirit, and although the weather was again bad, the sum of $1,047.78 was realized. Contributions to a large amount were received in response to the appeals of the ladies. The contributors were numerous, and from all parts of the country. We have only space to note the more important.

There was received, through Mrs. John R. Tucker, $50 from Gen. Joseph R. Anderson of Richmond, $50 from R. A. Robinson of Louisville, Ky., $25 from Gen. John Echols, $25 from Dr. Hunter H. McGuire, $50 from Joseph Bryan, Esq., of Richmond, $100 from Charles B. Rouss of New York, and $100 from Col. William P. Thompson; through Mrs. C. M. Figgat, $25 from Philip Sublett of Richmond, and $25 from Charles M. Fry of New York; through Miss Mary N. Pendleton, $100 from Major Lewis Ginter of Richmond, and $100 from Gen. G. W. C. Lee; $64.50, through Mrs. C. J. Brawley, from friends in Monroe city, Mo.; $30 from Miss Norma Stewart of Richmond, through Miss Belle White; Mr. May of New Orleans $50, through Miss Mary Lee; $103.75 from Buena Vista, through Mrs. Nichols and Mrs. Tucker; from Mr. L. J. McCormick $25, through Miss Sue W. Paxton; and $5 through Miss Glasgow; $35 from Mrs. E. G. Johns, through Mrs. J. K. Edmondson; Capt. J. P. Moore, $50; Judge James K. Edmondson, $100; M. M. Martin, $25; William A. Anderson, $50; and Thomas S. White, $50. As the reward of these efforts the ladies turned over to the Association the further sum of $3,308.31, making the total sum turned over by the Ladies' Association to the Jackson Memorial Association $8,388.93.

It is but just to say that but for the zealous, efficient and enthusiastic aid given by the ladies of Lexington the Jackson Memorial Association would have found it almost impossible to accomplish its work.

On the 17th of February, 1891, the following resolution was adopted by the Executive Committee:

" *Resolved*, that the Secretary communicate the following minute to Mrs. John A. Graham, president of the Ladies' Association:

" This Committee desires again to acknowledge its indebtedness to the ladies of the Jackson Memorial Association for the generous and valuable assistance which they have rendered to this Associa-

tion. The handsome sum realized through their persevering efforts
in conducting the recent bazaar will aid largely in completing the
patriotic work which we have undertaken, and entitle them to this
grateful recognition of their services."

On the same day a proposition was received from Col. R. Snowden Andrews in behalf of the Westham Granite Works proposing
to furnish the granite for the pedestal, and generously agreeing to
remit the usual ten per cent. allowed for profit. The proposition
was accepted. The granite was received in Lexington in July,
1891, over the Richmond and Danville Railroad and Chesapeake
and Ohio Railway, without charge for freight. The total cost to
the Association was $1,110.

When the cemetery was enlarged in 1880 a beautiful circle in
the centre was reserved as the final resting place of General Jackson's remains, and for the location of any monument that might
be erected to his memory. The trustees of the Presbyterian
church generously tendered this circle to the Association, and it
was accepted as the most suitable place for the monument. General Jackson had desired in his last moments to be buried in the
cemetery of the Presbyterian church in Lexington, of which he
was an officer, and to which he was so ardently attached, and as
the monument was to be over his grave it was considered that this
circle most appropriately fulfilled all the conditions.

It was determined to construct a vault under the pedestal for
the remains of General Jackson and his family. Accordingly
Prof. David C. Humphreys, C. E., of Washington and Lee
University, who designed the pedestal, was also selected to design
the vault. A plan was drawn for a vault under ground, with six
crypts, which might be increased in number, and was adopted. In
May work was commenced on the vault under the direction of
Mr. Edward J. Leyburn, and under the general supervision of
General Lee and Professor Humphreys. In the latter part of
June the remains of General Jackson and his daughter Mary
Graham Jackson who died in infancy, were quietly removed to
one of the crypts, and a few days afterwards the remains of his
daughter, Mrs. Julia Jackson Christian, were placed in another
crypt. The vault was completed and ready for the pedestal by
the last of June.

In the early part of July the blocks for the pedestal began to arrive, and were placed successively in position, and on the 11th of July the statue was removed and placed on the pedestal. The whole work was most successfully conducted by Mr. Leyburn, without accident or jar, and great credit is due to him for his skill and care. The statue was then veiled until the final unveiling on the 21st. The following description of the statue is taken from the *Rockbridge County News*, and is a better description than we could give:

"The location is in the beautiful cemetery on one of the commanding eminences around Lexington. Though it is in the City of the Dead, there is no suggestion of the sadness of the tomb about it. The site is beautiful and the prospect from it of mountain and valley is grand and majestic.

"It is in the midst of the scenes and scenery where Jackson in life loved 'to look through Nature up to Nature's God.' It is among his friends and those dearest to him in life. Around him in death's quiet bivouac sleep many of his bravest and most trusted soldiers.

"No more appropriate and fitting place for such a work could be conceived than in this quiet and now historic cemetery, which he chose as the last resting place for his remains.

"The sub-base and foundation of the monument is a vault, containing six chambers. These chambers are in two tiers of three each. The central one of the lower tier contains the body of Jackson and the central one of the upper tier that of Mrs. Julia Jackson Christian, his daughter. In the crypt with the father are the remains of Mary Graham, an infant daughter. This part of the structure is underground, and is surrounded by a slightly elevated grass mound out of which the monument itself rises.

"The statue itself is of bronze and is heroic in size. The figure is eight feet high and stands upon a bronze plinth eight inches thick. This rests upon a granite pedestal ten feet and six inches high, giving it from the ground to the top of the figure a height of nineteen feet two inches. The pedestal is noble for its simplicity and chasteness of style and fit adaptation to the rest of the work.

"It was constructed of Virginia granite from the Westham Granite Works, of Richmond, and weighs 31,550 lbs. The base

consists of four square graded slabs. Upon these rests a square
plain column, which is surmounted by a cornice.

" Upon the front side of the column is the simple inscription :

JACKSON,

followed by the dates ' 1824–1863.' On the obverse side is the
inscription :

STONEWALL.

The other two sides are blank.

" The figure faces southwest, and looks in the direction of the
line of the Valley. The *pose* of the statue is admirable. It stands
erect with the head bare and just sufficiently thrown back to repre-
sent a person watching a distant object. The weight of the body
is thrown in an easy and natural manner upon the left leg and is
supported by the left hand resting on the hilt of a sheathed sword
a little in the rear of the left side. The right leg is slightly bent
and that foot is a little advanced. In the right hand is a field
glass, carelessly resting on the right thigh as if just dropped into
that position from being used a moment before. The dress is a
Confederate officer's plain uniform with a Major General's insignia
of rank on the collar. The feet are encased in cavalry boots reaching above the knee. The sword is buckled on and the plate of the
sword belt has on it the Virginia coat of arms. The hilt bears the
letters U. S. The sword is modelled after one like that worn by
Gen. Jackson during the war, which was that of a United States
artillery officer.

" The conception of the whole figure is lifelike and natural. The
likeness is first-rate and the impression it gives is exceedingly
pleasant. The expression as a mere work of art has more life and
vitality about it than any bronze figure we have seen. The commanding posture and the keen and steady gaze impress the beholder
with the idea that Jackson is watching a charge or some other
important movement of his troops, and his satisfied and half pleased
look indicates that things are progressing satisfactorily. The statue
is a work worthy of the subject and of the artist.

" The sculptor is Edward V. Valentine, of Richmond, who
executed the recumbent figure of Gen. R. E. Lee, in Lexington,
which is regarded as the finest piece of work of its character on

JACKSON
1824-1863

the continent. A very cultivated Englishman who visited this country a few years ago declared that there was no recumbent figure in Great Britain that excelled it. Valentine also executed the statue of Gen. Breckenridge, at Lexington, Ky., and the busts of various other Confederate celebrities, among them those of Governor Letcher and Commodore Maury. Valentine was a pupil of the celebrated Berlin sculptor, Kiss."

The Executive Committee determined to make the unveiling ceremonies as imposing as possible. Lieutenant-General Wade Hampton was selected to preside on the occasion, Lieutenant-General Jubal A. Early as the orator, and the Rev. A. C. Hopkins, D. D., of Charlestown, W. Va., an intimate friend of Jackson and a chaplain in the Stonewall Brigade, to conduct the religious exercises. Col. Thomas M. Semmes, of the Virginia Military Institute, a pupil of Jackson, was invited to read some spirited odes suitable to the occasion. Major-General James A. Walker, who had commanded the Stonewall Brigade with such conspicuous gallantry, and was its only surviving commander, was selected as chief marshal. Preparations were made for the reception and entertainment of the large crowds that were expected. The Chairman of the Executive Committee sought to enlist the co-operation of the whole community both in town and county, and appointed the following committees ; how far he succeeded results will show :

On Decoration.—E. L. Graham, Chairman, and C. H. Effinger, William H. White, H. O. Dold, Jack Withrow, Hugh W. McCrum, G. B. Larrick, Benj. F. Wade, R. K. Godwin, B. H. Gorrell, Wm. G. McDowell, R. S. Anderson and John W. Barclay ; and the following ladies were associated and requested to act with this committee, namely : Mrs. Col. Nichols, Mrs. A. D. Estill, Miss Bessie Wharton, Mrs. Mattie Haskins, and Miss Annie R. White.

On Entertainment and Supplies.—John L. Campbell, Chairman, and J. P. Moore, Finley W. Houston, G. D. Letcher, M. W. Paxton, C. M. Figgat, W. C. Stuart, Wm. T. Shields, E. L. Perry, J. A. R. Varner, Thomas S. White, Tate Sterrett, S. O. Campbell, W. S. Hopkins, Frank T. Glasgow, H. H. Myers, E. M. Pendleton, R. E. Carter, S. R. Moore, E. H. Barclay ; and

the following persons were appointed outside of Lexington, namely:
John P. Welsh, Hugh Adams, Jr., John T. Wilson, Wm. Wade,
L. L. Watson, J. D. Anderson, R. R. Witt, Wm. F. Templeton,
J. J. L. Kinnear, R. K. Dunlap, C. J. Bell, J. S. Saville, A. M.
Monroe, Joseph M. Black, P. I. Huffman, John T. Dunlap,
Charles H. Paxton and Dr. G. B. McCorkle.

*On Reception of Supplies and Dispensing the same on the occasion
of the Unveiling Ceremonies.*—John P. Welsh, Chairman, and A.
W. Varner, Sam'l C. Charlton, John A. M. Lusk, E. N. Boogher,
C. R. Fox, Sam'l T. Ruff, Wm. B. Wallace, John W. Kelly, W.
L. Crigler, T. J. Crigler, John A. Jackson, Wm. Breedlove, Jas.
M. Senseney, J. V. Grimstead, Jayhugh Wills, C. H. Couch, John
A. Champ, Wm. Mitchell, Charles V. Varner, Charles Adams,
Wm. Seal, Wm. McKee, J. B. Holmes, F. T. Rhodes, Wm. A.
Rhodes, Wm. Hileman, J. E. Heck, E. R. Funkhouser, and such
others as the Chairman may call to his aid.

On Reception.—Col. E. W. Nichols, Chairman, and M. W. Paxton, W. G. McDowell, Reid White, Hugh McCrum, W. Geo.
White, Sandy P. Figgat, Ben. H. Gorrell, Jr., Edward R. Leyburn, Lewis M. Gibbs, J. A. Glasgow, J. Ed. Deaver, Fred. White,
A. A. Waddell, Percy Garing, and C. B. Anderson.

The Committees went vigorously to work and determined to
spare no efforts to make the occasion a great success. Capt. Jas.
J. White, J. C. Boude, and William A. Anderson were appointed
a Committee on Invitation. Invitations were extended to the Gov-
ernors of the Southern States, distinguished officers of the Confederate Army, and military and veteran organizations.

In response to the invitation the following letter was received
from a Committee of the Kentucky Veterans through General John
Echols:

"LOUISVILLE, KY., *July* 18, 1891.

"J. J. WHITE, J. C. BOUDE, W. A. ANDERSON, ESQS.,
    "*Committee of Confederate Association, Lexington, Va.*

"The members of the Confederate Association of Kentucky send
greeting to their brethren of Virginia, and give assurance of their
hearty appreciation of the sacred duty about to be performed and

cordial sympathy with the sentiment which inspires it. We reverently unite with them in the tribute rendered the memory of a patriot and hero, beloved of all the land for which he gave his life.

"Our comrades instruct us to thank you, in the name of all citizens of this Commonwealth who served or loved the Confederacy, for that which you do. All living Kentuckians know how great were the services, how sublime the virtues, of Thos. J. Jackson, and generations of this people yet unborn will honor and venerate his name.

"We are very truly,

" B. W. Duke,

" Reginald Thompson,

" Committee."

A. T. Barclay was appointed to arrange transportation on the railroads and William A. Anderson was placed in charge of the arrangements for the day.

The grounds and buildings of Washington and Lee University and of the Virginia Military Institute were generously placed at the disposal of the Executive Committee. A stand for the exercises, handsomely decorated, was erected upon the beautiful campus of Washington and Lee University, capable of holding the invited guests and distinguished visitors ; and seats were provided for as many as could be within reach of the orator's voice. The main buildings of Washington and Lee University, the barracks of the Virginia Military Institute, the Franklin Hall, Opera House, Court House, and the lecture room of the Presbyterian church where Jackson taught his colored Sunday school, were arranged as quarters for veterans and military organizations.

As the day approached it became apparent that the number in attendance would greatly exceed the highest number that had been previously expected. This stimulated the activity of the committees on supplies and entertainment, but they found a liberal response from the people of both town and country. During the preceding week large numbers came in to attend the unveiling ceremonies, chiefly those who had friends or relatives in town. On Monday trains came in at eight and twelve o'clock on the Chesa-

2

peake and Ohio Railway, and at five o'clock in the evening two
trains came in on the Baltimore and Ohio Railroad, all heavily
laden. Another large train on the Baltimore and Ohio Railroad,
due at nine o'clock, was delayed by a washout, and did not arrive
until daybreak the next morning. All was activity and bustle,
and the committees were busy receiving the strangers and pro-
viding quarters and provisions for the organized bodies.

The Stonewall Brigade and the unorganized veterans were placed
in the main buildings of the Washington and Lee University, the
Second Virginia Regiment of Volunteers and the Clarke Cavalry
in the barracks of the Virginia Military Institute, the Romney
Camp of Confederate Veterans in the Court House, the Winchester Camp and Rowan county (N. C.) Veteran Regiment in the
Opera House, and Lee Camp and its attendant camps, escorted by
the Richmond Light Infantry Blues, in the lecture room. The
basement of the chapel of Washington and Lee University was
reserved for the Maryland Line and Washington City Veterans,
who had not yet arrived.

UNVEILING CEREMONIES.

JULY 21, 1891.

The day opened bright, but cool and bracing. It had rained the evening before, but had cleared off. Fleecy clouds floated over the sky, and while obscuring the sun and cooling the atmosphere, created no apprehension of rain.

The people of the town were pleasantly aroused a little after daylight by the arrival of the Stonewall Brigade Band, who marched to the strains of martial music first to the statue of their beloved commander and then to their quarters at the Franklin Hall. The day was ushered in by a salute of fifteen guns fired by a section of the Rockbridge Artillery commanded by Col. William T. Poague, one of its captains. The guns used were a part of the cadet battery which Jackson used in drilling the cadets in artillery tactics, and constituted a part of the armament of the Rockbridge Artillery when it won immortal fame on the historic plains of Manassas just thirty years before. Trains soon began to arrive, heavily laden, on the Chesapeake and Ohio and Baltimore and Ohio Railroads, and continued to arrive until 12 o'clock. The number brought by the trains was variously estimated at from twelve to eighteen thousand.

But this was not all. All the roads leading to Lexington were crowded with people from the county, coming on foot, on horseback, in carriages, buggies, wagons and other vehicles improvised for the occasion. Whole neighborhoods were deserted, and it is believed that nearly one-half of the 20,000 population of the county outside of Lexington was in attendance. These brought large quantities of provisions to feed the veterans and visitors, and each party also brought a private lunch for themselves so as to save

23

the public lunches for the strangers. Large numbers also came in like manner from the adjoining counties of Augusta, Bath, Alleghany, Botetourt, Amherst and Nelson. The streets were lined with people, and large crowds assembled on the University campus. The crowd in attendance was variously estimated at from twenty to thirty thousand people.

The little town presented a holiday appearance. All the public buildings, business houses, and private residences were gaily decorated with bunting, festoons, and flags—the Confederate, the Virginia, and the Federal flag commingling. The cemetery was neatly trimmed and the graves of the Confederates handsomely decorated, a Confederate flag being placed at the head of each.

The tomb of General Lee in the University chapel was beautifully decorated under the direction of Miss Mary N. Pendleton. The main buildings of Washington and Lee University in front of the speaker's stand and the University chapel were prettily decorated, as well as the barracks of the Virginia Military Institute and Jackson's lecture room, with flowers, portraits and military emblems arranged with great taste under the direction of Miss Mercer Williamson. One of the most interesting objects was Jackson's old house, where he resided when he left for the army, ornamented by festoons and flags arranged with exquisite taste by Mrs. Nichols and Miss Annie White.

Arches with mottoes and legends spanned the streets at convenient distances. The one at the crossing of Main and Washington streets was of the mural-tower order. Over the keystone of the arch was a large Confederate flag, flanked by Virginia and Confederate battle flags. Along the crown of the arch on the obverse was

" WELCOME TO ALL WHO LIVE : TEARS FOR ALL WHO DIED."

On the reverse over the crown was the verse

> " From the field of death and fame
> Borne upon his shield he came."

The sides of the arch were ornamented with flags and shields and crossed swords, and muskets, and on the reverse were also portraits of Lee and Jackson.

Stretching across the street from the court house was a snow white banner bearing the words

"MARYLAND, MY MARYLAND,"

in honor of the Maryland line, and a square further up appeared in recognition of the North Carolina veterans,

"GOD BLESS OLD NORTH CAROLINA!"

Upon an airy and graceful arch in front of the public school building was seen an eagle perched, holding the motto,

"HAIL, VETERANS, HAIL."

But the grand arch was reached just before entering the cemetery. This was after the triumphal arch of Titus. Along the attic on the obverse, and between the dates 1824 and 1863, was the word "JACKSON," and underneath this, encircling the crown, "CHAN-CELLORSVILLE." Extending from top to bottom of the sides of the arch on the face were banners of the several Southern States, and between them the names of the battles in which Jackson fought. On the reverse in the attic was "STONEWALL BRIGADE," and the names of those who commanded it, as follows: "Jackson, Garnett, Winder, Baylor, Grigsby, Paxton, Walker, Terry."

The procession formed on the parade ground of the Virginia Military Institute, and, moving in front of the Institute, proceeded to the campus of Washington and Lee University, and rested in front of the speaker's stand. General Walker, Chief Marshal, and his aids, all of whom had served on the staff of Jackson's brigade, division or corps, rode at the head of the procession. Just as the exercises were about to begin the Maryland Line, accompanied by the Washington City Veterans, and headed by the Great Southern Band of Baltimore, forty pieces, arrived upon the ground and took its place in the line of procession.

Among the prominent people who occupied seats upon the platform were General Wade Hampton, the presiding officer; General J. A. Early, the orator; Rev. A. C. Hopkins, D. D.; E. V. Valentine, the artist; Col. T. M. Semmes, Gen. Fitzhugh Lee, Gen.

G. W. C. Lee, Gen. William H. Payne, Gen. L. L. Lomax, Gen. A. R. Lawton, Gen. John Echols, Gen. T. T. Mansfield, Gen. B. T. Johnson, Gen. J. R. Jones, Gen. Eppa Hunton; Gov. A. B. Fleming, of West Virginia; Lt.-Gov. J. Hoge Tyler; Major R. Taylor Scott, Attorney-General of Virginia; Lt.-Col. William McLaughlin, Col. James K. Edmondson, Capt. J. J. White, Capt. John M. Brooke, C. S. N., Hon. John Randolph Tucker, Rev. William F. Junkin, D. D.; Mr. Sewell Merchant, of Charlestown, West Virginia, General Jackson's orderly; Gen. Scott Shipp; Col. Thomas Smith, of Warrenton; Rev. J. William Jones, D. D.; Hon. A. M. Waddell, of North Carolina; Hon. H. St. George Tucker, Dr. S. B. Morrison, Col. C. T. O'Ferrall; Prof. T. M. Jackson, of West Virginia University; Hon. John W. Daniel, Judge John H. Fulton, Judge George G. Grattan, Col. R. Snowden Andrews, Col. A. W. Harman, Gen. John C. Shields, Capt. Thomas D. Ranson; Rev. George W. Peterkin, D. D., Bishop of West Virginia; and Hon. Wm. H. Crain, of Texas.

Mrs. Gen. Jackson, with her two grandchildren, Julia Jackson Christian and Thomas Jackson Christian; their father, William E. Christian, and Miss Christian; Capt. Joseph G. Morrison, Mrs. Jackson's brother; Mrs. Alfred I. Morrison; Miss Mary Lee; Miss Lucy Hill, daughter of Gen. A. P. Hill; Miss Daisy Hampton, daughter of Gen. Wade Hampton; Miss Heth, daughter of Gen. Henry Heth; and Mrs. Barney, of Fredericksburg, also occupied seats on the platform.

The exercises commenced by a selection played by the Stonewall Brigade Band. Lt.-Gen. Wade Hampton, who had been selected to preside, stepped to the front and was loudly cheered. When silence was restored he said:

"It was the custom of the great soldier in whose memory we are called together to invoke the Divine blessing on every undertaking, every duty he was called upon to perform. It was Stonewall Jackson's way, and, comrades, it is fitting that we should follow his noble example and invoke the blessing of the Almighty on what we do to-day."

He then introduced the Rev. A. C. Hopkins, D. D., of Charlestown, West Virginia, who offered the following prayer:

" Lord, our God, Thou only art infinite, eternal, and unchange-able. Thou, Most High, rulest in the kingdom of men and givest it to whomsoever Thou wilt. Not a sparrow falleth without Thee. In Thy kind providence these veterans are permitted to meet here to celebrate the character and achievement of the man who led them through hardship and battle to victory. Like him, who prepared for all action by prayer, we invoke Thy blessing upon these exer-cises, and as to Thee he ascribed the honor and power for victory, so to Thee we give thanks for our hero and his renown—for his greatness, most conspicuous in his goodness.

" Thou didst teach his hands to war and didst gird him with strength into the battle. Thou madest his feet swift as Asahel's. His name Thou madest an inspiration and tower of strength to his followers, a smiting and a terror to his enemies. In the industry and care of his preparations, in the fullness and accuracy of his calculation, in the certainty of his movements, in the might of his resistance we recognize Thy counsel and Thy hand. For the stead-fastness and intensity of his religion midst the temptations of cam-paign, camp and battle, we give Thee thanks. For his world-wide fame, spotless, untarnished and pure, we would render Thee our thanks. Thy hand has written his name imperishably among the world's great captains and thrown over it the halo of sanctity, that men may learn the beauty and power of Christian faith. When he had reached the zenith of his earthly glory, Thou didst call him higher into Thine own glory, and so didst veil his mortal eyes that he should not look upon the humiliation of defeat.

" And now we pray that the influence of his life may become immortal and universal ; that the people of the land he loved may learn from his example to pray and to believe, to fear God and to keep His commandments, and specially that his surviving comrades and their children may stand as a ' stone wall ' against all tides of social or political corruption, of moral decay and religious apostacy, unbelief or irreverence. So long as this monument shall stand its guard over his sleeping body and this statue look down upon the generations, may the world here catch the idea and the dimensions of the Christian hero—the patriot, the saint and the soldier. May the people of our whole land learn that ' righteousness exalteth a nation, but sin is a reproach to any people.' We ask Thy blessing upon the negro race, for whom he prayed and thought and labored, that they may acquire intelligence, morality and pure religion, and so become qualified for their new relations and duties, and for their higher obligations to God. ' A father of the fatherless and a judge of the widow is God in His holy habitation.' Protect and provide for all who were made orphans and widows by the casualties of war. We specially ask that Thou wilt amply provide and tenderly keep Thy handmaid to whom Thou gavest our leader in marriage, and from whom Thou didst take him. May she and her grandchildren be shielded from every unfriendly blast, and be enriched with all the blessings of a covenant-keeping God. Oh, Spirit of Grace! come, breathe effectually upon the heart and touch the lips of Thy servant who shall now speak to us of the Christian soldier, his comrade. Imbue him plenteously with the same grace that adorned the life he shall portray. Sustain him in the same faith and comfort him with the same hope."

Gen. Hampton then introduced Col. Thomas M. Semmes, Professor of Modern Languages and Rhetoric at the Virginia Military Institute, who, in a clear and impressive manner, read three selections of Confederate war poems, which appear below.

STONEWALL JACKSON'S WAY.

[Found on the body of a Sergeant of the Old Stonewall Brigade, at Winchester, Va.]

Come, stack arms, men ! Pile on the rails,
Stir up the camp fires bright ;
No matter if the canteen fails,
We'll make a roaring night.
Here Shenandoah brawls along, ·
There lofty Blue Ridge echoes strong,
To swell the Brigade's rousing song,
Of "Stonewall Jackson's way."

We see him now !—the old slouched hat ·
Cocked o'er his eye askew—
The shrewd, dry smile—the speech so pat,
So calm, so blunt, so true.

The "Blue Light Elder" knows them well.
Says he, "That 's Banks—he 's fond of shell—
Lord save his soul !—we 'll give him "—well,
That 's " Stonewall Jackson's way."

Silence ! Ground arms ! Kneel all ! Caps off !
Old Blue Light 's going to pray.
Strangle the fool that dares to scoff!
Attention ! it 's his way.
Appealing from his native sod,
" In forma pauperis," to God—
" Lay bare thine arm ; stretch forth thy rod."
Amen ! That 's Stonewall's way.

He 's in the saddle now ! Fall in !
Steady—the whole brigade !
Hill 's at the ford cut off ! We 'll win
His way out, ball and blade.
What matter if our shoes are worn !
What matter if our feet are torn !
" Quick step—we 're with him ere the morn,"
That 's Stonewall Jackson's way.

The sun's bright lances rout the mists
Of morning, and, by George,
There 's Longstreet struggling in the lists,
Hemmed in an ugly gorge.
Pope and his columns, whipped before.
" Bay'nets and grape ! " hear Stonewall roar ;
" Charge, Stuart ! Pay off Ashby's score ! "
Is Stonewall Jackson's way.

Ah, maiden ! wait and watch and yearn
For news of Stonewall's band.
Ah, widow ! read with eyes that burn
That ring upon thy hand.
Ah, wife ! sew on, pray on, hope on ;
Thy life shall not be all forlorn—
The foe had better ne'er been born
Than get in " Stonewall's way."

SLAIN IN BATTLE.

[From Breechenbrook, by Mrs. Margaret J. Preston.]

" Break, my heart, and ease this pain ;
　Cease to throb, thou tortured brain ;
　Let me die, since he is slain—
　　　　　　Slain in battle !

" Blessed brow, that loved to rest
　Its dear whiteness on my breast,
　Gory was the grass it prest—
　　　　　　Slain in battle !

" Oh ! that still and stately form,
　Never more will it be warm ;
　Chilled beneath that iron storm—
　　　　　　Slain in battle !

" Not a pillow for his head ;
　Not a hand to smooth his bed ;
　Not one tender parting said—
　　　　　　Slain in battle !

" Straightway from that bloody sod,
　Where the trampling horsemen trod,
　Lifted to the arms of God—
　　　　　　Slain in battle !

" Not my love to come between,
　With its interposing screen ;
　Naught of earth to intervene—
　　　　　　Slain in battle !

" Snatched the purple billows o'er,
　Through the fiendish rage and roar,
　To the far and peaceful shore—
　　　　　　Slain in battle !

" Nunc dimitte—thus I pray ;
  What else left for me to say,
  Since my life is reft away ?—
                    Slain in battle !

" Let me die, O God ! the dart
  Drinks the life-blood of my heart.
  Hope and joy and peace depart—
                    Slain in battle !"

"OVER THE RIVER."

By J. Daffore.

[Dr. Hunter McGuire thus concludes his account of the last moments of Stonewall Jackson : "Then his manner changed, and he murmured, ' Let us pass over the river, and rest under the trees.'"]

" Over the river, over the river,
    There where the soft-lying shadows invite ;
  And fanned by the south wind the forest leaves quiver,
    And fire-flies dance through the sweet summer night.

" Soldiers and comrades ! we 'll cross that broad river,
    Far from the tumults of trumpet and drum,
  And the cannon's deep boom, and the fierce squadron's shiver,
    As they reel in their saddles. Then come, brothers, come.

" Over the river, over the river,
    Come ere the sun-goeth down in the west ;
  Angel forms beckon us ; sent to deliver
    The weary from labor—to offer him rest.

" Over the river, a fathomless river,
    In the land where no shadow is needed nor seen,
  Where the leaves of the forest trees wither, no, never,
    And the fruits are all golden, the pastures all green.

" From the couch where the warrior lay stricken and dying
   He saw in a vision the country so fair ;
All its streams and its valleys, its mountains outlying,
   And the city whose gates are of pearls rich and rare.

" Over the river, the dark-flowing river,
   Death bore the hero and victor and saint ;
Great in earth's conflict, and greater than ever
   When they had left him all bleeding and faint.

" Waiting to cross it, all radiant with glory,
   Strong in the faith which is born of pure life ;
Bequeathing a name to the record and story
   That tells of bold deeds in the patriots' strife."

The reading was followed by music, and Gen. Hampton then introduced Lt.-Gen. Jubal A. Early, the orator of the day. As the General's bent form, clothed in Confederate gray, arose, another mighty cheer went up. He spoke as follows :

ADDRESS OF GENERAL EARLY.

My Friends and Comrades, Ladies and Gentlemen:

We are assembled here for the purpose of manifesting our respect and admiration for one of the most illustrious men and grandest characters that have figured in the annals of history, and it is with a sincere apprehension of my inability to render an adequate tribute to his memory that I appear before you on this occasion.

Thomas Jonathan Jackson was born in northwestern Virginia in the year 1824. His military career began in 1842, when he was admitted as a cadet at the Military Academy at West Point. He graduated in 1846, and was appointed a brevet second lieutenant in an artillery regiment in the United States Army. His first service in the field was in the Mexican war, where he was engaged in artillery service under General Scott, from Vera Cruz to the City of Mexico. He participated in all the actions on that line, displaying such courage and energy as to be twice brevetted for his conduct, his last brevet being that of Major of Artillery.

In 1851 he received the appointment of Professor of Natural and Experimental Philosophy and Artillery Tactics in the Military Academy at this place, and resigned from the Army to accept it. That position he filled until 1861. When the secession of the Southern States took place, and Abraham Lincoln, in violation of the fundamental provisions of the Constitution and the eternal principles of liberty, declared war against the seceding States, Virginia took her stand with her sister States of the South. Major Jackson, like all true Virginians, stood by his native State, and devoted his energies and his life to her service. His first service was to conduct the corps of cadets to Richmond, in the

33

latter part of April, for the purpose of aiding in drilling and instructing the volunteers who were being mustered into the service of the State under the supervision of General Lee. On the 27th of April he was appointed by Governor Letcher a colonel in the Virginia service, and ordered to take command at Harper's Ferry, which had been abandoned by the Federal authorities after attempting to destroy the stores and machinery at that point. Colonel Jackson found the place occupied by some militia and volunteers, of whom he took command, which he retained until General Joseph E. Johnston was assigned to the command in the Valley in the latter part of May.

Very soon thereafter a brigade of Virginia regiments was organized, and Colonel Jackson assigned to its command. This was the brigade which afterwards became distinguished as the "Stonewall Brigade." On the 17th of June Colonel Jackson was commissioned a Brigadier-General in the Confederate service, but still remained under the command of General Johnston. About this time Harper's Ferry was evacuated by General Johnston, as Patterson was moving with a considerable force from the north, and McClellan was reported as moving from the west to unite with him. But before the evacuation took place the railroad bridge across the Potomac was destroyed, and a considerable quantity of ordnance stores and machinery was sent to the rear.

After some manœuvring of the troops under General Johnston, which had been organized into four brigades, commanded respectively by Generals Jackson, Bee, Bartow and Colonel Elzey, General Jackson had some fighting with a part of Patterson's army, which had crossed the Potomac, near Falling Waters, on the second of July. This was his first engagement, and in it only a very small portion of his force was engaged, though Patterson reported he had repulsed "10,000 rebels." General Jackson's loss was much lighter than that of the enemy, and he retired in good order before a much larger force than his own. From this time the Army of the Valley, under General Johnston, was mainly occupied in manœuvring until it moved to the assistance of General Beauregard's Army at Manassas, against which McDowell had advanced with largely superior numbers. That movement began on the 18th of July, and General Jackson's brigade was in the advance.   It reached Manassas about night on the 19th, having come by rail from a station on the Manassas Gap railroad.   The other troops came later, a portion not arriving until the day of the main battle.

McDowell had been making demonstrations with his troops for several days, out of which grew the affair at Blackburn's Ford on the 18th.

On the 21st, just as Generals Johnston and Beauregard were preparing to carry out a plan of attack devised by the latter, McDowell made an attack on our extreme left which rendered a change of operations necessary.   A large portion of McDowell's army crossed Bull Run above our left, and assailed Evans's brigade on the flank.   This brigade, assisted by a portion of Cocke's brigade, held the enemy in check for some time, until Bee's brigade came to its assistance.   The enemy's force, however, continued to increase to such an extent that Bee's men were giving way when General Jackson arrived with his brigade and arrested the further progress of the enemy.   It was while General Jackson thus held the attacking force at bay, and Bee's men were giving way, that the latter, in order to encourage his men, exclaimed to them, "There is Jackson standing like a stonewall. Rally behind the Virginians."   From that expression the cognomen of "Stonewall" was given to General Jackson, and under it he will be known for all ages.   The appellation, however, is not very characteristic of him as a soldier.   It is true that just at that time he was standing like a stonewall against the overwhelming numbers of the enemy, and so stood until other troops were brought up that turned the tide of battle, and sent the enemy flying from the field ; but his subsequent career showed that he was more like a thunderbolt of war than a stonewall.   During the action he had received a very painful wound in his left hand, but he gave no indication of it until the battle was over, when he sought the necessary surgical aid.   From that day, just thirty years ago, the sobriquet of "Stonewall Jackson" became familiar throughout all the Southern States, and will be remembered for all time to come.

I do not wish to be understood as giving to General Jackson the entire credit for the victory at Manassas.   He occupied a subordinate position, and went into action under the orders and supervision

of the two generals whose forces had been united for the occasion ;
but he performed the duty assigned him with great skill and
courage, thus enabling his superiors to bring other troops into
action and secure the victory which ensued.

The two armies were now united under the command of General
Johnston, and on the seventh of October General Jackson was
appointed a major-general in the Confederate service. He was
subsequently assigned to the command of the Valley District, and
assumed it in November. To give a full account of his Valley
campaign would require a well-sized volume, and I can only give
a brief sketch. The main object of his presence there was to pre-
vent the accumulation of heavy forces under McClellan, who had
succeeded McDowell, by the appearance of threatening the safety
of Washington. This duty he performed most admirably by his
bold movements and demonstrations, though his force was quite
small. His first engagement was at Kernstown just south of Winchester, on the 23d of March, 1862. His presence in the valley
had caused the accumulation of heavy forces of the enemy there
under Shields and Banks. After considerable manœuvring during the fall and winter of 1861–2 in the lower valley, he had
retired to Mt. Jackson, and the enemy had occupied Winchester.
Learning that the enemy had detached a considerable force for the
purpose of crossing the Blue Ridge and operating on Johnston's
left, he marched from Mt. Jackson on the 22d of March, and on
the next day attacked a part of Shields's force at Kernstown. The
fight was maintained for some time, but such heavy reinforcements
were brought up by the enemy that General Jackson was finally
compelled to retire, but he did so in good order, and only fell back
to the vicinity of Newtown, where he made a stand, and the enemy
did not dare to attack him. He retired to Woodstock on the next
day, and on the first of April he retired to Rude's Hill, a little
north of New Market. General Jackson's force at Kernstown did
not exceed 3,000 men, while that of the enemy was at least thrice
as great; yet the movement had the desired effect of preventing
any troops being sent to the aid of McClellan, and causing a body
of troops which had already started to be returned.

General Jackson remained at Rude's Hill until the 17th of
April, confronted by a heavy force under Banks on the opposite

hills. In the meantime McClellan's army had been carried by
water to the Peninsula, and General Johnston's army had moved
back for the purpose of confronting the former, leaving Ewell's
division on the Rappahannock. General Jackson now fell back to
Harrisonburg, being timidly pursued by Banks. From Harrisonburg General Jackson moved to Swift Run Gap in the Blue Ridge,
and Ewell having been ordered to that point with his division,
General Jackson moved his own division across the Blue Ridge to
the Virginia Central Railroad, and then along the line of that road
by Staunton to unite with the brigade of General Edward Johnson, which had retired from the Shenandoah Mountain upon the
advance of a considerable force under Milroy.

The two forces having united they advanced against Milroy,
and defeated him on the 8th of May at McDowell. After pursuing
Milroy for a considerable distance General Jackson returned to the
valley with his own and Johnson's troops, for the purpose of
uniting with Ewell and attacking Banks, who had retreated to
Strasburg. The junction with Ewell was made on the 21st of
May in the Luray valley, and on the 23d he attacked a considerable force at Front Royal, driving it across the Shenandoah in the
direction of Winchester, the greater portion of which force was
captured by a body of cavalry under Colonel Flournoy, with considerable stores and two ten-pound rifle guns.

On the next day, the 24th, portions of Banks's army were found
retreating on the turnpike from Strasburg to Winchester, and
attacked and dispersed, a number of wagons and a quantity of
stores being captured, but the main body of the army had passed
on to Winchester. On the 25th General Jackson attacked Banks's
army at Winchester and utterly defeated it, capturing some three
thousand prisoners and an immense quantity of stores. Banks
had made his escape before his army was routed, and the latter
was pursued by a body of cavalry until it crossed the Potomac.
On the 28th General Jackson moved towards Harper's Ferry, and
arrived at Halltown a short distance from that place on the 29th,
a small force of the enemy having been driven from Charlestown
on the march. Here it was ascertained that Shields had been
ordered to move from the east of the Blue Ridge with a considerable force, and Fremont with another from the South Branch of

3

the Potomac to Jackson's rear, so as to cut off his retreat, and he therefore moved on the 30th in the direction of Strasburg, where it was expected the two forces of the enemy would meet. He made a rapid march, and on the 31st reached Strasburg, just in time to escape Fremont's force from the west, Shields having also arrived at Front Royal from the east. On the first of June he moved up the valley from Strasburg, followed by Fremont's army, until he reached Harrisonburg, where he turned off to Port Republic. On the 8th, Ewell's division, which had been left at Cross Keys to confront Fremont, was attacked, but repulsed the enemy. Shields's army had moved up on the east side of the south fork of the Shenandoah, as the bridges over that stream had been burned, and on the 9th it was attacked and defeated by a portion of General Jackson's troops, retreating down the way it had come. Fremont's army had moved up to the river on the 9th, but it could not cross as the bridge over it had been burned, and he retreated down the valley on the 10th. Thus ended Jackson's campaign in the valley, and by his operations there he had so bewildered the authorities at Washington as to cause a heavy force of at least 40,000 men under McDowell to be detained from McClellan's army in order to protect that city, in addition to the troops which had been employed against himself.

Very soon thereafter General Jackson began his movement towards Richmond in order to coöperate with General Lee's army in the attack on McClellan's, and his army reached the vicinity of Richmond on the 25th. He participated with great energy and skill in the seven days' battles which sent McClellan's army in retreat to the protection of gunboats at Harrison's Landing on James River, thus relieving the City of Richmond of the danger of capture which had been threatening it.

It being impracticable to attack McClellan's army at his "new base" on James River except at great disadvantage, General Lee's army, including Jackson's command, returned to the vicinity of Richmond for the purpose of rest, and to be convenient to needed supplies.

A new commander of Federal troops, Major General John Pope, had now appeared in northern Virginia, east of the Blue Ridge, at the head of an army styled the "Army of Virginia,"

and composed of the corps of McDowell, Banks and Fremont, the
latter then being commanded by Sigel. Pope, on assuming the
command, had declared, in very bombastic style, that he had come
from the West, " where we have always seen the backs of our
enemies," and he declared that his " headquarters would be in the
saddle." General Lee sent General Jackson with his own division
of four brigades and Ewell's of three brigades to look after the
redoubtable warrior. Ewell's division reached Gordonsville about
the middle of July. Jackson's division soon followed, and General Jackson himself arrived on the 19th. Robertson's brigade of
cavalry and an independent company of cavalry were added to the
command, and about the last of the month A. P. Hill's division
arrived to reinforce General Jackson. In the meantime there had
been some skirmishing with portions of the enemy's cavalry which
crossed the Rapidan on reconnoitering expeditions. General Jackson's whole force did not exceed 20,000 officers and men for duty,
while the force under Pope in the field considerably exceeded
40,000, there being in and near Washington other troops, while
Burnside had a considerable force at Aquia Creek near Fredericksburg.

Having been informed that a portion of Pope's army was at
Culpeper C. H., on the sixth of August General Jackson decided
to advance against it, with the hope of defeating it before reinforcements could arrive. The movement was begun on the 7th, the
route taken being through the county of Madison. On the 9th a
portion of Pope's army was encountered on Cedar Run near
Slaughter's Mountain, in Culpeper, and defeated after a brisk
engagement, the enemy being pursued a mile or two when fresh
troops were encountered which had just arrived. The pursuit now
ceased, as it had become dark, and there was a halt for the night.
The next morning a reconnoissance made by the cavalry under the
charge of General Stuart, who had arrived on a tour of inspection,
disclosed the fact that the greater portion of Pope's army had
arrived, and the rest was coming up. General Jackson, therefore,
did not deem it prudent to push the pursuit further. The next
day Pope sent a flag of truce requesting permission to bury his
dead, and it was granted ; something over six hundred of his dead
that were lying on the field being buried on that day. On the

night of the 11th Jackson's force commenced retiring, carrying off one piece of artillery and over five thousand muskets that had been captured on the field, and it returned to its former position near Gordonsville.

Pope had now begun to see something more of the "rebels" than their backs, and the very presence of General Jackson in the vicinity of Gordonsville had so bewildered the minds and excited the fears of the authorities at Washington that, on the 3d of August, a peremptory order was given for the evacuation of Harrison's Landing, and the reinforcement of Pope by McClellan's army. On the 14th, in response to a frantic direction from Halleck, McClellan telegraphed:

"Movement has commenced by land and water. All sick will be away to-morrow night. Everything done to carry out your orders. I don't like Jackson's movements. He will suddenly appear when least expected."

Having ascertained that McClellan was sending troops to reinforce Pope, General Lee, on the 13th, ordered General Longstreet, with his division, D. R. Jones's division, two brigades under General Hood, and Evans's brigade, to Gordonsville. General Stuart was ordered to the same vicinity with Fitz Lee's brigade of cavalry, and General R. H. Anderson was ordered to follow Longstreet with his division. Longstreet having arrived General Jackson's command was moved in the direction of Somerville Ford on the Rapidan, on the 15th, and camped some three or four miles from the ford. General Lee having arrived and assumed command a forward movement was commenced on the 20th. Pope, whose army was in Culpeper, between the Rapidan and Rappahannock, having learned the intended movement from a dispatch to Stuart, which was captured by a party of his cavalry, had hastily retired across the Rappahannock. General Jackson crossed at Somerville Ford on the 20th, and bivouacked near Stevensburg in Culpeper. Longstreet crossed the Rapidan lower down and moved to the vicinity of Kelly's Ford on the Rappahannock. Each command was preceded by a brigade of cavalry, which severally encountered portions of the enemy's cavalry, and drove them across the Rappahannock. On the 21st a forward movement was commenced for the purpose of crossing the river and attacking Pope's army, but

the enemy appearing in heavy force at the point where it was pro-
posed to cross, it was determined to seek a crossing further to the
left. On the 22d General Jackson moved to a point opposite the
Fauquier Sulphur Springs, Longstreet taking position to cover the
ford at the railroad bridge and the crossings above, so as to mask
General Jackson's movement to the left. On arriving opposite
the Springs it was found that a force of cavalry, which had retired
on the appearance of Jackson's advance, had burned the bridge at
that point. It was now nearly night, and a regiment of Lawton's
brigade and two batteries of artillery were crossed over the ford at
the Springs, while my own brigade crossed over a dam about a
mile lower down. It was intended that other troops should cross
at the same point, but night coming on the crossing was deferred
until morning. During the night a heavy storm burst upon us,
and the rain poured down in torrents. The next morning the
Rappahannock was out of its banks, and the further crossing was
rendered impossible.

My brigade was moved to the vicinity of the Springs under
directions from General Jackson, and I took command of all the
troops on that side. General Jackson was having the bridge
repaired as soon as possible in order to cross over other troops, but
it took longer than was expected. In the meantime very heavy
bodies of the enemy's troops were discovered moving up from
below, and taking position opposite that occupied by my brigade.
Stuart had crossed the river above the day before and made a raid
with a part of his cavalry into Pope's headquarter train, capturing,
among other things, Pope's dispatch book, which disclosed the
fact that McClellan had evacuated Harrison's Landing, and a portion of his army had already joined Pope. Late in the afternoon
the enemy made an advance against my position, but the movement was thwarted by a judicious use of artillery, in which a
battery that had arrived with two or three regiments of cavalry
under General Robertson, who had been with Stuart on his raid,
rendered efficient service. It having become apparent that the
greater part of Pope's army had arrived in the vicinity of the
Springs during the night, it was determined to withdraw the force
with me on that side, and, as the recrossing began but a short time
before day, and the artillery had to be carried by hand over the

bridge, which had been but partially repaired, it was daylight before the last of the troops with me recrossed. Just as they did so the enemy's infantry was discovered advancing in line, with skirmishers in front, and the corps of Sigel, Banks and Reno (lately arrived from Burnside's army) soon passed over the very ground we had occupied.

On the 23d Pope had telegraphed Halleck : "The enemy's forces on this side, which have crossed at Sulphur Springs and Hedgeman's river, are cut off from those on the other side. I march at once with my whole force on Sulphur Springs, Waterloo bridge and Warrenton, with the hope to destroy these forces before the river runs down."

As the dispatch book captured by Stuart disclosed the fact that a portion of McClellan's army had already joined Pope, that the remainder was to be sent to him over the Orange and Alexandria railroad, and that a body of troops under Cox from the Kanawha valley was being brought over the Baltimore and Ohio railroad for the same purpose, General Lee determined to send General Jackson to the rear of Pope to break the railroad, and thus separate him from the approaching reinforcements, and to follow with Longstreet's command as soon as General Jackson was well on his way. Here was a conception worthy of the greatest strategists of ancient or modern times, not excepting the great Napoleon in his palmiest days, and General Jackson undertook its execution with that promptness and energy which always characterized him without the slightest cavil as to its feasibility or any request that he be allowed to reconnoiter.

The necessary orders having been given the day before, early on the morning of the 25th General Jackson moved with his command, crossing the river at Hinson's Mill, some miles above Waterloo Bridge, and then passing Orlean bivouacked his command for the night near Salem in Fauquier county. All baggage wagons had been left behind, and no vehicles were allowed except ordnance and hospital wagons and ambulances, the men carrying three days' cooked rations in their haversacks. Resuming the march early on the 26th the column, accompanied by a portion of Stuart's cavalry, moved through Thoroughfare Gap in the Bull Run Mountain, and passing Gainesville, the head of it, preceded by Munford's regiment of cavalry, reached Bristoe station on the Orange and Alexandria railroad by night. A company of cavalry and a company of infantry found there were soon disposed of, and two trains coming from the direction of the Rappahannock were captured, one having escaped. Trimble's brigade and also a portion of cavalry under Stuart were dispatched to Manassas Junction, where eight guns, with their horses, equipments, and ammunition complete, immense commissary and quartermaster stores, a considerable number of tents, and over three hundred prisoners were captured. The station at Bristoe was occupied by the three brigades of Ewell's division left after Trimble was detached, and the other divisions, Hill's and Jackson's, bivouacked in the vicinity. The next day Ewell's three brigades were left at Bristoe station to guard the approach from the direction of Warrenton Junction, with directions to retire in the direction of Manassas if a superior force advanced against him, as it was not desired to bring on a general engagement at that point. Hill's and Jackson's divisions were moved in the morning to the Junction. Soon after their arrival a body of infantry arrived on a train from Alexandria, and, having gotten off the train, moved towards the Junction for the purpose of driving off the supposed "raiding party." It was met by the fire of two batteries and some of Hill's infantry, and driven back and pursued for some distance, the train on which it arrived being captured and destroyed, as was the railroad bridge over Bull Run. The railroad bridge over Kettle Run, south of Bristoe Station, was destroyed, and the track from that point to the station torn up by a portion of Ewell's command. The bridge over the Run north of the station was also destroyed, as were the two captured trains.

Pope at first supposed this was a mere cavalry raid, but he soon found out his mistake, and found it necessary to look out for his line of retreat. He had now been joined, besides the reinforcement from Burnside, by Reynolds's division of Pennsylvania Reserves, Heintzelman's and Porter's corps from McClellan's army, and Riatt's brigade of Sturgis's division from Washington, if not by other troops. His force of infantry and artillery must therefore have numbered at least 75,000 effectives without counting his cavalry.

In the afternoon of the 27th a considerable force, which came from the direction of Warrenton Junction, and proved to be Hooker's division of Heintzelman's corps, moved across Kettle Run against Ewell's advanced regiments at Bristoe. One or two columns, apparently of brigades, were driven back, when the enemy commenced moving to our right over open ground beyond the range of our artillery. The force which came in view was evidently much larger than the force Ewell then had. He, therefore, in accordance with his instructions, ordered a withdrawal of his force, which was accomplished in good order and without any loss, the force retiring to Manassas. During the night Jackson's division, under General Taliaferro, moved with all the trains of the command on the Sudley road, across the Warrenton turnpike, to the vicinity of the battlefield of first Manassas, and Gen. A. P. Hill moved with his division to Centreville. Early on the morning of the 28th General Ewell moved with his division across Bull Run at Blackburn's Ford, and then up the Run to the vicinity of the old stone bridge, where he crossed over and joined Jackson's division. Hill's division subsequently, on the same day, came up from Centreville, and the whole command was united northwest of the Warrenton turnpike, and facing it. These movements had been covered by portions of the cavalry, and were designed to mislead the enemy, in which object there was perfect success. During the night of the 27th Stuart set fire to the cars and the stores at Manassas that could not be carried off, and they were destroyed amid a terrible explosion of shells that were in some of the cars.

On the 27th Pope commenced the movement of his troops to the rear for the purpose of looking after his line of communications. McDowell's and Sigel's corps moved along the Warrenton turnpike in the direction of Gainesville, while the other corps moved on the right towards Bristoe and Manassas. Longstreet had crossed the river at Hinson's Mill on the 26th, and followed the same route taken by General Jackson; Anderson, who had arrived with his division, having relieved Longstreet on the south bank of the Rappahannock. Longstreet's advance reached Thoroughfare Gap on the morning of the 28th, where a part of McDowell's force was posted to dispute his passage. He succeeded, however, in forcing a passage, and a part of his command passed through the Gap that evening. From Gainesville McDowell's and Sigel's corps had moved in the direction of Manassas on the 28th, to which point the main body of Pope's troops were converging, as he expected to find General Jackson's force there and destroy it. But the bird he expected to trap had flown, and Pope then directed his troops to move on Centreville.

In moving towards Manassas McDowell had his left flank on the turnpike, and this fact having been discovered by some skirmishing a portion of General Jackson's command had with it, the General, supposing it was moving towards Centreville, prepared to attack it, but discovering that it was turning off in the direction of Manassas before reaching his front, three brigades of his own division and two of Ewell's were moved to the right and formed into line facing the turnpike. Just before sunset a column of the enemy was discovered moving along the pike, when the three brigades of Jackson's division and the two of Ewell's advanced to the attack. An obstinate and sanguinary engagement ensued, which lasted until dark. At the close of the engagement both sides held their ground, the enemy, consisting of King's division of McDowell's corps, which was bringing up the rear of the left of that corps, having been heavily reinforced. My own brigade and that of Hays, under Colonel Forno, were ordered to advance just before the close of the action, but by the time they reached the field the darkness which had ensued and the nature of the ground prevented a further advance. During the night King's division retired. Generals Ewell and Taliaferro were both wounded in this action, the former having to suffer amputation of a leg. General Lawton succeeded to the command of Ewell's division, and General Stark to that of Jackson.

Early on the morning of the 29th, the enemy began to approach in heavy force from the direction of Manassas and Centreville. When the enemy's movements began to be developed, General Jackson arranged his line so as to conform to them. His own division, under Stark, was posted on the right, two of Ewell's brigades, under Lawton, occupied the centre, and Hill's division the left, the whole being posted behind a railroad grade of an unconstructed road which ran through a considerable body of woods.

The batteries were posted in some fields behind ridges in rear of
the right and left flanks. My own brigade, and Hays's under
Colonel Forno, with a battery of artillery, were posted under my
command about a mile in the rear of the right of the line, on a
ridge which commanded a view of the turnpike in front and large
fields between it and the turnpike. A considerable force had been
reported as advancing from Manassas towards Gainesville, threatening our right flank and rear, and my orders were to watch that
force and hold it in check, as well as to keep open communication
with Longstreet's command, which was known to be approaching
from the direction of Thoroughfare Gap.

The manœuvring of General Jackson after he got on Pope's
line of communications to the rear, upon the approach of the
enemy, furnishes an exhibition of what is known as "grand tactics," which is unsurpassed in the annals of war. By his movements he had completely baffled Pope's efforts to crush him with a
vastly superior force, and bewildered him as to his locality until
he had placed his command in a strong position, where it could be
joined by Longstreet's approaching forces and the army be thus
reunited under General Lee, who was accompanying Longstreet.

But Pope was not the only one who was mystified on this occasion, as the authorities at Washington were as greatly bewildered
as he was, and were terribly frightened by apprehension of danger
to the safety of that city.

The enemy commenced his attack early on the morning of the
29th by opening a heavy fire of artillery on General Jackson's
right, which was vigorously responded to by our batteries on that
flank, which were moved to the front for that purpose, when a
fierce cannonade ensued that lasted for several hours. The enemy
also pushed columns of infantry on our left into a body of woods
that bordered on the railroad grade all along that portion occupied
by Hill's troops. Then ensued a good deal of desultory fighting
on that part of the line with Sigel's corps, which was finally driven
from our front about noon.

In the meantime, about or a little before 11 a. m., the head of
Longstreet's command, composed of Hood's two brigades, was
seen advancing along the turnpike in my front, in line of battle,
and the rest of the command soon came following close in the rear,

when the whole command commenced taking position on both sides of the turnpike and to the rear of Jackson's right.

It being apparent that the purpose for which I had been posted at the position I occupied had been completely subserved by the interposition of Longstreet's command between me and the force of the enemy reported to be advancing from the direction of Manassas, and that there was no further need for my presence there, I determined to withdraw, without waiting for orders, and moved to the left where the fighting was going on and there was need for the services of the troops under me. Hays's brigade was at once sent to the left to rejoin the division, and as soon as two of my own regiments, which had been posted in front beyond the turnpike, were withdrawn, I moved to the woods in rear of the centre of our line and reported to General Lawton.

In the afternoon the enemy concentrated large bodies of infantry in the woods in front of Hill's position, and after a fierce artillery fire from numerous batteries on that flank, which were responded to with effect by Hill's batteries, the enemy's columns of infantry advanced against the position occupied by Hill's brigades, when a fierce and obstinate engagement, or rather series of engagements, ensued, which lasted until late in the afternoon, the enemy being repulsed in all of his attacks, as was an attack on our right.

The seventh and last attack was made by the enemy about or a little after 4 p. m., when a column of the enemy succeeded in crossing the railroad grade near the centre, because the two brigades there stationed had retired a little to the rear as their ammunition was exhausted. On being informed of this fact, I moved to the front with my brigade, with the 8th Louisiana Regiment, of Hays's brigade, on my left, and the 13th Georgia, of Lawton's brigade, on my right, and drove the enemy in confusion across the grade, my command pursuing beyond it for some distance before it could be stopped. This was the last attack on Jackson's line on the 29th, and the enemy had been defeated in all of his attacks. The troops engaged in these attacks in the afternoon were the corps of Heintzelman and Reno, supported by Reynolds's division on their left. Sigel's corps had been so badly worsted in the forenoon that it was not able to unite in those attacks.

General Lee had ordered Longstreet to attack the enemy's left on his arrival about noon, but the latter, according to his own statement, had insisted on taking time to reconnoiter. A number of his batteries, however, were posted on a commanding position between his troops and Jackson's right, and engaged in the artillery duel with those of the enemy.

About sunset General Longstreet ordered Hood to advance with his two brigades, supported by Evans's, along the turnpike and attack the enemy, but before Hood moved he was himself attacked by a column of the enemy which was moving along the turnpike in the direction of Gainesville. This proved to be King's division of McDowell's corps which was moving in advance of the corps along the turnpike to cut off Jackson's retreat, under the hallucination that the latter had been defeated. King's division encountered Hood just as he was about to move forward, and a sharp action ensued, the enemy being driven back and pursued for some distance, when the darkness compelled Hood to halt. He returned to his former position about 12 o'clock at night, and thus ended the fighting on the 29th, our troops remaining masters of the field on every part of it.

On the morning of the 30th our troops occupied the positions they held at the close of the battle of the day before, with some slight shifting of the brigades along the railroad grade not necessary to mention. There was some skirmishing in the forenoon along Jackson's line, especially on the left, but there was no assault at that time, the enemy being held at bay. There was also some artillery firing on the right, which continued until the afternoon. At noon Pope issued the following order to his troops:

"August 30th, 1862, 12 m.

"The following forces will be immediately thrown forward in pursuit of the enemy, and press him vigorously during the whole day. Major General McDowell is assigned to the command of the pursuit.

"Major General Porter's corps will push forward on the Warrenton turnpike, followed by the divisions of Brigadier Generals King and Reynolds. The division of Brigadier General Ricketts will pursue the Haymarket road, followed by the corps of Major General Heintzelman; the necessary cavalry will be assigned to these columns by Major General McDowell, to whom regular and frequent reports will be made. The general headquarters will be somewhere on the Warrenton turnpike."

In the afternoon there was a slight change in the programme, and Porter's corps, supported by King's division, advanced against Jackson's right, and Heintzelman's and Reno's corps, supported for a time by Ricketts's division, advanced against the left. The assaults began about 3 p. m., and were very fierce and determined, especially on the right where Jackson's division was posted, but were met with equal determination. There were at least three assaults on Jackson's division, following each other in succession, which were repulsed, some of the men of the brigades commanded by Stafford and Johnson using stones when their ammunition was exhausted. Longstreet's batteries, by a well-directed fire on the left flank of the attacking columns, contributed largely to their repulse. The assaults on the left were also fierce, but were successfully resisted by Hill's brigades.

R. H. Anderson's division had arrived during the forenoon, and joined Longstreet's command; and finally, about 4 p. m., after the last attack on Jackson's right had been repulsed Longstreet ordered his infantry to attack the enemy's left, and his troops moved forward with Hood in the lead closely followed by Evans. They were rapidly supported by Anderson's division and the brigades under Kemper, D. R. Jones and Wilcox.

The enemy was assailed with great vigor, and was steadily driven before Longstreet's advancing lines from successive positions which he occupied. General Jackson's command had also advanced at the same time in pursuit of the troops that had been repulsed, and some of Hill's brigades encountered and engaged a part of the retreating forces on the left, which they pursued to Bull Run, capturing a number of pieces of artillery. Jackson's and Ewell's divisions did not become engaged with the enemy in the pursuit. Longstreet's command continued to press the enemy on the right until his whole army was driven across Bull Run, when darkness put an end to the pursuit. This command captured several batteries of artillery.

The cavalry, under Stuart and Fitz Lee, had rendered valuable services during all of the operations against Pope, and near the close of the battle of the 30th, General Robertson, with a portion of his cavalry, attacked and routed a body of the enemy's cavalry on the extreme right.

At the close of the battle we were masters of the entire field ; and, in the series of battles on the plains of Manassas, we had captured more than 7,000 prisoners, besides 2,000 wounded left on our hands, thirty pieces of artillery, upwards of twenty thousand stand of small arms, a number of regimental colors, and a considerable amount of stores. Our own loss in killed and wounded was 7,224, including a number of valuable officers.

Pope's army retired to Centreville on the night of the 30th, where it was reinforced by Sumner's and Franklin's corps of McClellan's army and some other troops.

In his report Pope claims that he was confronted by greatly superior numbers on our part. The Confederate soldier, though ragged, barefooted, and often hungry, had a wonderful faculty of multiplying himself on the field of battle, so as to present the appearance of "overwhelming numbers" to a frightened enemy. This was especially the case when Stonewall Jackson was about.

On the 31st, Longstreet, with his command, including Anderson's division, was left on the battle-field to engage the attention of the enemy, and cover the burial of the dead and the removal of the wounded, while General Jackson moved his command across Bull Run at and below Sudley Ford, for the purpose of turning the enemy's right and intercepting his retreat. Moving to the left over country roads, we reached the Little River turnpike, leading from Aldie past Germantown and Fairfax C. H. to Alexandria, late in the afternoon, and after moving on that road for a short distance we bivouacked for the night. On the next morning (1st of September) the march was resumed, Hill's division being in the advance. At Ox Hill, near Chantilly, a large force of the enemy was encountered in the afternoon, which had been moved out in that direction to cover Pope's retreat along the turnpike from Centreville to Fairfax C. H. Hill at once attacked the enemy with a part of his division, and Ewell's division also moved up and became engaged. There was a sharp conflict which lasted until near night, during which time there was a severe thunderstorm, and two of the Federal generals, Kearney and Stevens, were killed. At the close of the fight we held possession of the field, and the enemy retired during the night. Longstreet's command came up at night after the action had closed.

The next morning it was discovered that Pope had now learned the art of retreating so well that it was impracticable to intercept him, and he was permitted to take refuge in the fortifications of Washington without further molestation. In a few days he was relieved from his command and sent to the Northwest to look after the Indians in that quarter, so that he never again had the opportunity of looking at the backs or faces of the " rebels."

In the campaign against him, General Jackson's force did not at any time exceed 20,000 men, and when Longstreet and Anderson arrived their combined forces did not exceed 25,000 men, and, after the reunion of the two forces on the 29th of August, the whole army under General Lee, including the cavalry, did not exceed 50,000, if it reached that number. Pope's army, after the arrival of the reinforcements from McClellan's army and other sources, must have approached very nearly 100,000 men before the arrival of the corps which joined him at Centreville after the battles of the 29th and 30th.

In this campaign against Pope General Jackson displayed greater ability and resources than on any other occasion, because the circumstances by which he was surrounded required such display, and he fully justified the confidence reposed in him by General Lee.

There have been criticisms of the strategy displayed by General Lee in sending General Jackson to the rear of Pope, thus dividing his army and placing the smaller portion between two hostile forces of greatly superior numbers. This is said by some military critics of the red tape order to have been a blunder and in violation of the rules of war. If so it was a very successful blunder. Genius is trammelled by no arbitrary rules, but is able to burst the fetters which bind ordinary intellects. General Lee thoroughly understood Pope and fully appreciated General Jackson. In a letter to General Fitz John Porter, written in July, 1870, in response to an inquiry, he said : " I had no anxiety for Jackson at 2d Manassas. I knew that he could hold on till we came, and that we should be in position in time."

I have thus given at some length a detailed account of the operations in which General Jackson was for the greater part left to act according to his own promptings, as they serve to demonstrate his great energy and ability.

The divisions of D. H. Hill and McLaws, two brigades under J. G. Walker, and Hampton's brigade of cavalry, which had been left near Richmond, and were ordered up after the evacuation of Harrison's Landing, reached the army after the battles of the 29th and 30th of August.

General Lee now determined to cross the Potomac into Maryland, and on the 3d of September General Jackson commenced the march and reached Frederick City, in Maryland, on the 6th. I will here say that Whittier's poetic story about Barbara Fritchie has as little foundation in fact as Buchanan Read's account of Sheridan's poetic ride.

On the 15th General Jackson, having crossed the South Mountain at Boonsboro Pass and the Potomac at Williamsport, and moved to the vicinity of Harper's Ferry, in coöperation with McLaws and Anderson, who had gained Maryland Heights, and J. G. Walker who had reached Loudoun Heights, both commanding Harper's Ferry, compelled the surrender of the enemy's force at that point, about 11,000 prisoners being received and paroled, and 12,000 stand of small arms, seventy pieces of artillery, and a very large amount of stores, provisions, wagons and horses secured.

The command of Longstreet and D. H. Hill's division, after an attack on the latter at Boonsboro Pass by the Federal army now under the command of McClellan, having taken position at Sharpsburg, where they were confronted by McClellan's army, composed of his own and Pope's army, General Jackson crossed the Potomac early on the 16th, with his own and Ewell's division, and participated in the fighting on the 16th and 17th. His command, occupying the left of our line in the woods where is situated the Dunkard or Tunker church, did some of the heaviest fighting in that battle, repulsing all the attacks of the enemy though made by overwhelming numbers. The last attack by the enemy was made on our right and was repulsed by the division of A. P. Hill which had just arrived from Harper's Ferry, where he had been left to finish paroling the prisoners and to secure all of the arms and stores captured.

On the 18th our army confronted McClellan's the whole day without any renewal of the engagement, and on that night we began to recross the Potomac into Virginia, the last of the troops effecting the crossing after sunrise on the 19th.

A small body of the enemy having crossed the river on the night of the 19th, were driven back on the 20th by A. P. Hill's division.

In the battle of Sharpsburg, or Antietam, as the enemy call it, General Lee's whole force did not exceed 35,000, infantry, artillery, and cavalry ; McClellan states his as a little over 87,000, while he estimates our strength as more than 97,000, which latter estimate he makes mainly on some statements by Banks, who always saw doubly when Stonewall Jackson was about.

The army of General Lee remained in the Valley until November, watching the movements of McClellan, and in the meantime the army was divided into two corps, General Jackson being made Lieutenant-General on the 11th of October and given command of one corps, while Longstreet with the same rank was given command of the other corps. In the early part of November McClellan was relieved of the command of the Federal army and it was given to Burnside.

Burnside having commenced a movement to take possession of Fredericksburg, General Lee's army moved in that direction to thwart him, taking position on the south side of the Rappahannock, while the enemy occupied the Stafford Heights. Jackson's corps extended down to Port Royal, while Longstreet's occupied the heights in the rear of and above the town.

On the 11th of December Burnside threw pontoon bridges across the river and crossed his army over into the town and the flats below.

General Jackson's whole corps having been moved up took position on our right extending down to Hamilton's crossing, below the town. On the 13th heavy attacks were made on our line by

4

the enemy, both on the right and left, and were repulsed, the heaviest fighting being on Jackson's line, where the enemy was repulsed with heavy loss after he had gotten possession of parts of the line. The attack was not renewed on the 14th or 15th, and on the night of the 15th the enemy recrossed the river to the opposite side.

Our army now resumed its former position, Jackson's right extending to Port Royal again.

Burnside was subsequently removed from the command of the Federal army and General Hooker became his successor. Longstreet had been sent south of James River with two of his divisions, Hood's and Pickett's, to operate against the enemy in that quarter.

On the 29th of April, Hooker, whose army had been increased to a little over 130,000, crossed a large force over the river several miles above Fredericksburg and advanced to Chancellorsville. At the same time a considerable force was crossed over below the town. Before this, General Jackson's troops had been moved up to the vicinity of the town from below, and when General Lee ascertained that a heavy force had crossed the river above the town, he moved three of General Jackson's divisions and the two divisions of Longstreet's corps that were present up to meet that force, leaving the former division of Ewell, to the command of which I had succeeded, and Barksdale's brigade of McLaws's division with several batteries of artillery under my command, to watch the force that had crossed below. As soon as the force at Chancellorsville was encountered, a vigorous attack was made on it and it was placed on the defensive. Hooker's force at this point had been increased to a little over 90,000 men, while our force there was about 46,000. General Lee, after consulting with General Jackson, determined to make a flank movement with the three divisions of the latter, by moving around to Hooker's right flank and rear and attacking it. The conduct of this movement was given, of course, to General Jackson, who took charge of it. It was successfully made on the 2d of May, and General Jackson was advancing with the attack when, by a deplorable mistake, he was shot and mortally wounded by some of his own men. The movement was subsequently successfully made under the charge of

General J. E. B. Stuart, and the enemy driven from his position towards the river. After a good deal of manœuvering and fighting below, the enemy was compelled to retreat across the river on the night of the 5th. A brilliant victory was thus achieved, mainly by the success of the movement which was begun by General Jackson. The rejoicing over that victory, however, was marred by his death, which occurred on the 10th, and a gloom was cast over the entire Confederacy.

In his report of the battle, General Lee says : "The movement by which the enemy's position was turned, and the fortunes of the day decided, was conducted by the lamented Lieutenant-General Jackson, who, as has already been stated, was severely wounded near the close of the engagement on Saturday evening. I do not propose here to speak of the character of this illustrious man, since removed from the scene of his eminent usefulness by the hand of an inscrutable but all-wise Providence. I nevertheless desire to pay the tribute of my admiration to the matchless energy and skill that marked this last act of his life, forming as it did a worthy conclusion of that long series of splendid achievements which won for him the lasting love and gratitude of his country."

What can I say to add to that tribute to his memory? Generals Lee and Jackson fully appreciated the characters of each other, and there was the most perfect harmony between them. No man in all the land felt more keenly the loss of his great coadjutor than General Lee. When any one desires to find a defense of the justice of the cause for which they fought, let him point to the characters of Generals Lee and Jackson. And I conclude now with the declaration I have made before : I trust that every faithful soldier of the Army of Northern Virginia is ready to exclaim with me : "If ever I disown, repudiate, or apologize for the cause for which Lee fought and Jackson died, let the lightnings of heaven blast me, and the scorn of all good men and true women be my portion!"

The exercises were closed with the benediction by the Rev. Dr. Hopkins.

THE PROCESSION.

At 1 o'clock the roll of a dozen drums called the old veterans and the volunteers to their positions, and with great rapidity the line was again formed, and the march in the direction of Jackson's monument, one half mile distant, was resumed. The long and brilliant procession was composed as follows:

MAJOR GENERAL JAMES A. WALKER, *Chief Marshal.*

Aids.

COL. H. KYD DOUGLASS,	MAJ. RANDOLPH BARTON,
MAJ. R. W. HUNTER,	MAJ. GEO. G. JUNKIN,
CAPT. J. P. SMITH,	CAPT. J. G. MORRISON,
CAPT. JOHN T. SAYERS,	S. H. LETCHER.

Assistant Marshals.

COL. S. J. C. MOORE,	COL. D. H. LEE MARTZ,
COL. C. T. O'FERRALL,	COL. WILLIAM A. MORGAN,
CAPT. H. R. GARDEN,	CAPT. JAMES BUMGARDNER,
CAPT. J. A. McNEAL,	CAPT. S. W. PAXTON,
CAPT. JOHN CARMICHAEL,	CAPT. J. H. H. FIGGAT,
CAPT. J. P. MOORE,	CAPT. B. C. RAWLINGS,
M. D. WILSON,	J. T. DUNLAP,
W. F. JOHNSTON,	H. E. MOORE.

The Stonewall Brigade Band.
The Rockbridge Artillery, 65 men, accompanied by a contingent of Carpenter's battery ; Col. William T. Poague commanding.

The surviving veterans of the Stonewall Brigade, with some veterans from other brigades, 600 men, Col. Andrew Jackson Grigsby, whose dauntless courage had been displayed on so many battlefields of the war, commanding, and accompanied by the Martinsburg and Harrisonburg bands.

Grand Confederate Camp of Virginia, as follows, Col. W. P. Smith, commander, and staff (mounted) :

R. E. Lee Camp of Richmond, 125 men, with a detachment of the Washington Artillery of New Orleans, Col. Booker commanding, preceded by Richmond Light Infantry Blues as escort, 48 men, Capt. Sol. Cutchins commander, accompanied by Light Infantry Blues band and R. E. Lee Camp drum corps.

Buchanan-Pickett Camp of Norfolk, 60 men, Capt. T. S. Garnett commanding, preceded by Fourth Regiment band ; Stonewall Camp of Portsmouth, 30 men, Capt. Wood commanding.

R. E. Lee Camp of Hampton, 30 men, Capt. Segar commanding.

R. E. Lee Camp of Alexandria, 25 men, Col. Smoot commander.

Winchester Camp No. 4, composed of veterans from Frederick and other Valley counties, 225 men, Capt. E. Holmes Boyd commander, preceded by Winchester band.

Survivors of Clarke Cavalry, 6th Virginia Cavalry, 40 men, Maj. H. L. D. Lewis commander.

William Watts Camp of Roanoke, 50 men, Col. S. S. Brooke commander ; accompanied by Sidney Johnston Camp, sons of veterans, 30 men ; preceded by Roanoke Machine Works band.

Romney Camp, 41 men, Capt. G. W. Finley commander.

Society of Army and Navy of Maryland, 300 men, Gen. G. H. Steuart commanding ; preceded by the Great Southern band of Baltimore, 40 pieces.

Rowan County, North Carolina, Veteran Regiment, Lieut.-Col. J. A. Ramsey commanding ; 65 men, and 25 sons of veterans.

2d Regt. Virginia Volunteers, Col. J. A. Nulton commanding ; preceded by 2d Regiment and Woodstock bands, and represented by the following companies, each containing about 32 men : Woodstock Guards, Capt. Baker commanding ; Winchester Light Infantry, Capt. Trenary commanding ; Harrisonburg Guards, Capt. Roller commanding ; Roanoke Light Infantry, Capt. Rives commanding ; Jeff. Davis Rifles of Salem, Capt. Strouse commanding ; Pocahontas Guards, Capt. Lewis commanding ; Toms-brook Company, Capt. Flemming commanding.

The Lynchburg Volunteers, accompanied by a drum corps, comprising :

Virginia Zouaves, 25 men, Capt. Craighill commanding ;

Home Guards, 25 men, Capt. Camm commanding ;

Fitz Lee Troop (dismounted), 23 men, Capt. Ingram commanding ;

Light Artillery Blues (without guns), 26 men, Capt. Dillon commanding.

Veterans of First Va. Cavalry, 40 men, mounted, Maj. Charles F. Jordan commanding.

Students of Washington and Lee University with University banner.

Citizens on horseback and in carriages.

Following came carriages containing the orator, presiding officer, chaplain of the day, and sculptor ; Mrs. Jackson, her two little grand-children, Julia Jackson Christian and Thomas Jackson Christian, W. E. Christian and Miss Christian ; ladies of the Jackson Memorial Association, the Executive Committee of the Association, distinguished officers of the Confederacy, and distinguished guests.

The procession marched up Main street, and as it passed the cemetery gate the Rockbridge Artillery filed to the left, and moving through the cemetery took their position at their guns in the rear of the cemetery.

The following graphic description of the unveiling is taken from the Rockbridge County *News:*

" The procession marched around and to the rear of the cemetery by the way of the Fair Ground road, and was massed in a field south of and about three hundred yards distant from it. As the head of the column reached the given point it halted, and a line was formed coming to a front face. Then another line was formed in close order in the rear of this, and so on until a solid phalanx was formed—a phalanx of veterans as brave, too, as ever stood invincible on Greece's historic fields. The volunteers stood in the rear. This done they awaited the unveiling. The troops and the cemetery were each on opposite hills, and each well in view of the other.

"In the meantime the people had filled the cemetery grounds, and the carriages with Mrs. Jackson and her little grandchildren and the distinguished gentlemen and honored visitors of the occasion had arrived. Beside the statue was erected a little platform upon which those who were to do the unveiling might stand and could be seen.

"A few minutes before the last of the soldiers had filed in, which was to be the signal, Mrs. Jackson, the wife, and little Julia Jackson Christian, aged five years, and Thomas Jackson Christian, aged three years, the grandchildren of "Stonewall" Jackson, mounted the steps. Mrs. Jackson is a matronly lady, with a pleasant face and a quiet, dignified manner. Her appearance would not at all indicate that she had been a widow twenty-eight years. The little children are sweet little prattlers with blue eyes and curly yellow hair. They are pretty children, and would be so pronounced without regard to any sentiment connected with their lineage. They were neatly dressed in white, and were bareheaded during the ceremonies. Whilst waiting they conducted themselves with a good deal of childish playfulness. The little one especially showed a disposition to pull the string before the time, and his grandmother had to watch his little hands very closely.

"When the signal gun sounded the two little children with united hands pulled the cord and let the veil fall, and this grand statue of the great Jackson was unveiled to the admiring gaze of the thousands around it. The cannoneers of the old Rockbridge Artillery at the foot of the hill announced the event with fifteen guns, from the cannon which they used at First Manassas, and a shout such as these quiet precincts never before heard, rent the air. It was answered by the veterans on the other side with an old-fashioned 'rebel yell.' The reverberating hills took it up and echo carried it into the deep recesses of the blue mountains, where it died away into sweet musical cadences, and was lost in the distance. The armed infantry fired volleys till it sounded like a real battle was in progress.

"As the battery ceased firing, Gen. Walker again put his column in motion. They passed down and in at the rear of the cemetery, and along the broad pathway by the statue, and out at the main entrance. As the old veterans approached the statue they gazed upon it as it were with reverence, and as they passed saluted. Some were heard to say, 'That is old Jack.' One stopped and looked intently upon it, and solemnly said, 'This is Jackson,' and passing his hand over his eyes was heard to mutter, 'May God preserve it,' and marched on. The bands that at first approached played 'Dixie,' and excited a little cheering, but the vast crowd was remarkably serious looking. The last bands which came played solemn tunes."

The procession returned to the University campus, some dropping out as they passed their quarters, where it dispersed.

INCIDENTS OF THE PROCESSION.

We are again indebted to the Rockbridge County *News* for incidents of the procession :

"As the procession advanced the stalwart and soldier-like form of Gen. Walker was everywhere recognized, and he was repeatedly cheered.

"The surviving veterans of the Stonewall Brigade marched in simple civilian's dress and yet were no less objects of universal interest and applause. The brigade marched in order of the regiments which composed it. The 2d, Col. Nadenbousch commanding, had a large representation of veterans from the counties of Berkeley and Jefferson. The 4th was commanded by Adjutant William Wade and was well represented. The 5th, under its old commander, Col. J. H. Williams, had hardly less than 200 men in line from Augusta. The representatives here from the 27th were largely Rockbridge men with a few from West Virginia, and with the 33d were commanded by Capt. Frank C. Wilson, of the 27th.

"Many companies got the few men that represented their old contingent and marched together, it may be said, for the last time. Borne at the head of the 27th by Sergeant R. S. McCartney, of Union, was a historic flag. It was the flag of that regiment which he carried just 30 years before that day at its head at the battle of the first Manassas. It is of silk and scarred and faded, but it is a beautiful piece of handiwork, and evidently the work of some fair daughters of the Confederacy. Sergeant McCartney wore in the parade an old Confederate uniform worn by him in the army. In

61

the centre of the brigade, on a beautiful Kentucky horse, rode its commander, Col. Andrew Jackson Grigsby, of the 27th. He sat erect as an arrow. His face and form looked emaciated, but he had a vigorous bearing. He wore a long, flowing, gray beard, and a full suit of gray hair was brushed back from his forehead, and he was attired in an unpretentious suit of gray. From the time he entered Main street at Henry until the procession was dismissed, he bore his white hat in his hand above his head, and as he advanced looked neither to right nor left. One of his soldiers remarked of his old commander that he had again the light of battle in his eye. He was a unique and striking figure, and attracted widespread attention.

"The veteran camps from the eastern part of the State were uniformed in gray and with their fine bands of music and handsome escort, the Richmond Light Infantry Blues, were a very imposing part of the parade.

"The mountain veterans from Romney, and the numerous contingent from the valley represented in the Winchester camp, were, like the Stonewall Brigade, in civilian's dress, but their familiar record of valor assured for them a hearty welcome along the line. Borne aloft by veterans from Woodstock was a tattered battle flag which had been at first Manassas. Upon it was 'Muhlenburg Rifles, July 21, 1861.'

"The most beautiful spectacle presented by the veteran organizations was by the Marylanders. In their columns were upheld three historic Confederate battle flags.

"The North Carolina men were distinguished by the large white helmets which they wore. On Virginia's soil they had often displayed heroic valor, and all rejoiced at their presence here on Tuesday.

"The volunteer soldiers, with their bright uniforms and shining arms, added vastly to the effect of the procession.

"A pleasant remembrance of this procession is that every company and organization received a full share of the honest and hearty welcome and applause.

"The recognition of Mrs. Jackson and her grandchildren aroused much enthusiasm."

We add the following from the Washington *Post*:

" Right in front of the stand S. M. Bosworth, of Beverly, W. Va., raised proudly aloft a bullet-torn battle-flag, presented to the Thirty-first Virginia Regiment by General Jackson, at West View, when the army was reorganized. It was carried all through the war, from the battle of McDowell on the sixth day of May, 1862, to the battle of Fredericksburg, Va., on the 13th of December, 1863, when it was given to Mr. Bosworth's sister for safe-keeping. The color-bearer who carried it at Sharpsburg fell dead with his head blown off by a shell, but the soldiers picked the flag out of his blood, and to-day, all smoke-begrimed and stained and torn, it waved under the sunshine of a peaceful sky."

Free lunch had been prepared at the Public School building, Franklin Hall, the gymnasium of the Washington and Lee University, and the mess-hall of the Virginia Military Institute, for veterans and strangers, of which thousands partook. Every private house was thrown open and bountiful lunches spread, to which the invited as well as uninvited, especially veterans, were equally welcome. Few if any went away unfed or dissatisfied. To add to the comfort of the crowd huge barrels of ice water were placed on the University campus and along the streets, which were constantly replenished, more than 3,500 pounds of ice having been used.

Good order and good humor prevailed, and all seemed to be delighted with the day. The trains soon commenced to leave and thousands hied their way homewards. Many remained over night and were handsomely entertained by the citizens and the committee, and left the next morning with their haversacks well filled. Many lingered, and it was several days before all the strangers had left. Thus closed the most eventful day in the more than a century of Lexington's existence. Such a day is not likely to occur for another century !

CONCLUSION.

The Executive Committee had little left to do. Its work practically ended with the unveiling ceremonies. The Committee, however, met on the 23d to close up its business.

Col. Edmondson, the chairman, through the town papers, acknowledged the fidelity and ability with which the several committees, to wit: John L. Campbell, chairman, and his associates; John P. Welsh, chairman, and his associates; E. L. Graham, chairman, and his associates, and Col. E. W. Nichols, chairman, and his associates, had discharged their labor and duty in connection with the preparation for the unveiling exercises of the 21st instant.

The committee passed resolutions thanking Mr. E. J. Leyburn for the fidelity and efficiency with which he discharged the duty of superintending the erection of the pedestal and monument; Prof. D. C. Humphreys, C. E., for his valuable services generously given by him to the Association in connection with the designing and erection of the pedestal and vault; Charles M. Figgat, Esq., for his faithful and valuable and efficient services as treasurer of this Association from its organization to the completion of its work; and the Chesapeake and Ohio Railway Company, through Decatur Axtell, vice-president, and the Richmond and Danville Railroad Company, through Edmund Berkeley, superintendent, for generously remitting all charges for the transportation of the stone from the quarries to Lexington.

The Committee audited their accounts and after paying all bills found they had a balance to their credit in the Bank of Lexington of $974.88. After paying for a railing around the monument and for this publication they expect to have a balance of $500, which

64

they propose to invest so as to have an income for contingencies and for the preservation of their work. They do not propose to disband, but will preserve their organization for the care and protection of their sacred trust.

This sketch would be incomplete if it did not bear testimony to the zeal, enthusiasm, and energy shown by Col. James K. Edmondson, chairman of the Executive Committee, which contributed so much to the success of the enterprise, and to whose executive ability the success of the unveiling ceremonies was so greatly due.

And now the Committee have accomplished their pious work, which has engaged their anxious care for the last eight years—how well let others judge. They think they have erected a worthy and fitting memorial of their illustrious commander.

But Jackson needed no monument to perpetuate his fame. His fervent piety, religious zeal, and stern devotion to duty will place him in history alongside the noblest heroes of Christendom ; while his military career, in boldness of conception, celerity of movement, and successful achievement, rivals those of the greatest soldiers of ancient or modern times.